In a Beginning there was

Majik

Jeff Cross

ISBN 978-0-9825793-1-2

Copyright © 2009 by Jeff Cross

Printed in the U.S.A.

J Cross Books
www.jcrossbooks.com
Papa's Library

Preface

In an age before the Dark Ages, before iron and steel, before gods were invented, there was a practice thought to be a gift. It was an ability which some came by naturally and others unnaturally. In later years it became known as Majik. This ability has changed over the centuries—how it is used, how it is derived and even how it is thought of.

The characters included in this book, though fictional, travel a very real path learning the very origins and even shaping and changing how magic was used and developing the basis of how it is viewed today. As the world grows older, the places the power resides change. It is obvious that the power, or magic, is still here.

The language used to manipulate the magic has long since past. The church uses a language similar to this dead language, but it isn't the same, and the results are different. People are different, the world is different, and the goals have changed. People are no longer in tune with their environment. The world has been through many changes.

This accounting tells of the many lives and the changes they effected upon the Majik, and the land, and possibly you.

Contents

I

Stranger

Streets paved with leaves, gold intermingled with hues of yellow and red, stretched out in every direction from the town common. They fluttered and moved like waves on a lake with the gusty breeze. The sun was a finger's width above the western horizon. Long shadows from the low buildings seemed to dance on the leaf strewn lanes. A hooded figure stood motionless, facing into the breeze. His gray woolen robes rustled about the ankles of his leather traveling boots. A gloved hand lazily grasped the four cubit high walking staff, ornately carved on the thick end with runes and glyphs. The uppermost part of his staff flowed seamlessly into a detailed carving of an acorn about the size of an average lemon. The entire oaken shaft was as black as night from age.

A hearty laugh came from the whitewashed building to the man's right. The small painted sign above the door identified the business as the local pub and eatery. Two young men stumbled out of the door, turned into the wind, and headed up the street. They laughed and talked loudly as they leaned on each other to maintain their balance. The figure turned and walked toward the door.

Upon his entering the pub, all eyes turned and tried to peer beyond the hood to glimpse a face. A nearby table became silent as the occupants stopped smiling. A tall thin man at the serving bar stopped speaking to the barman. He looked like a trader with

1

various trinkets strewn on the bar before him and some hanging strategically from his pockets. The barman was a large man, with his sleeves pushed up above his elbows and he had on a vest, which he was unable to fasten. He wore a smile as if it were the only expression he knew. The trader was expressionless and, after a glance, turned back to the barman but didn't speak.

As the traveler continued to the bar, the barman said, "Good eve, friend, would you care for a warm mead?"

Without saying a word the traveler laid a copper on the bar as the barman drafted the mead from the barrel behind him. Taking the mug, he turned and eased into the darker end of the room and sat with his back to the wall. Everyone understood the stranger was not there for conversation. They each returned to their own.

A little while later another man entered and joined the two men at the table across the room. The barman's wife came in from the rear living quarters with some fresh cleaning rags and a replacement candle for the stranger's table. As she approached the table and without introduction she said, "I have a veil stew if you would like some."

The stranger respectfully slid the hood off and nodded. "The mead is good," he said. He lifted the empty mug off the table.

She lit the candle, nodded at him with a smile, and taking the mug, turned and exited the room.

The dark-haired man looked to be in his fifties. His hair was pulled back and tied near the top of his neck. His eyes were dark as if the pupils extended to the outer edge of the iris. The rest of his features were strong, yet average. His expressionless face told a story of long adventures past and close calls.

A few minutes later the barman's wife delivered a large wooden bowl of stew, half a loaf of bread, and a fresh mug of mead. The stranger smiled, thanked her, and began the meal.

The door opened again and a large farmer entered with a boy of fifteen. It was obvious that the boy was his son as the resemblance was uncanny. As they stood near the door, allowing their eyes to adjust, they took in the entire tavern. The farmer's eyes stopped on the stranger, then he greeted the three men at the table, grasping forearms with each as was the custom.

They moved to the stranger's table and spoke. "I am Hym, son of Jaak. This is my son, Taam, of whom I'm very proud. Are you Loy?"

"Yes," said the stranger as he stood and grasp Hym's forearm. "Please sit with me and break bread. We have much to discuss."

Both man and boy sat, and the barman's wife approached with an ale and a buttermilk. She greeted both as friends and offered stew. They accepted and settled down comfortably.

"I thank you for the interview," said Hym. "Once I recognized the gifts, I could think of nothing more important than an education for my son."

The stranger welcomed the comment as the thick farmer shook off his overcoat. "Describe the occasion when you first saw a gift was present," said Loy.

"It was a day of rest," said Hym, "so we went to sit on the riverbank. It was in the mid-spring between planting and hoeing, and we were in a relaxed spirit. We sat and talked and picked out shapes in the clouds as we lay splayed in the grass. Then I recalled that I was to fetch some fish from the market for my wife. I said to Taam that we'd have to hurry to make the market before the fisher went his way for the night. But as we rose, Taam spoke to the river. 'Share your bounty sister,' he said, 'and I shall remove a dam of your choice.' I felt he spoke as if to jest, but four large bass leapt from the water and into the grass beside us. We were both surprised and thanked the river for the bounty.

"Three days later we were hunting near the river. We came upon a natural dam where some old trees had hung and were diverting the water, changing the course of a tributary. It made us think of his oath. Then four fish leapt in the air in front of the log jam. My son said, 'I must remove this blockage myself.' He labored almost an hour dislodging the boughs. He would not accept my help. When he was done, four more fish leapt on to the bank."

He sat looking at Loy with a proud grin and then began eating. Loy had made no expression throughout the tale.

Loy looked at the boy. "Why do you think this happened, Taam?"

Taam sat looking at him. Of all the questions he could ask me, why this? he wondered. I've not even thought of why. What should I say so as not to destroy my chance of the education Father wants for me?

4

Then he realized what he wanted to say. "I meant it. I mean, I wasn't jesting with the river." Waiting nervously for a reply he added, "Is that why, sir?"

Loy ignored the question. "Do you understand what your father is asking?"

"I think," Taam said, "the advanced ones teach the most gifted youth the secrets of magic so they then become advanced themselves. They can do magic and travel around teaching and healing people."

Loy looked at farmer with an expression of astonishment. Hym said nothing. Loy looked back at the farmer's son. "Taam, the title 'advanced ones,' is not a title used lightly, for I do not consider myself an advanced one. I am a teacher and I am a student. The education your father wants for you is a lifetime commitment. This means you would not be an honored farmer as your father is. It is evermore growing dangerous for people like us, as heretics become more radical each year." Loy paused for a moment. "As for magic, everyone uses magic. Magic is a broad term and could be called by other names, such as knowledge or science. Starting a fire would be magic to someone who had never seen fire before."

He looked at Hym. "The purpose of an apprenticeship is much more in depth than what Taam believes. All living things must obtain a balance in life, a balance within themselves and with their surroundings. Upon obtaining this balance one can then begin to experience things far beyond those who do not achieve a balance. Reaching this goal is not without its costs. Some die at a very young age, some even worse. As his father, you must understand that you and your wife may never see him again."

Hym looked from his son to Loy and back again. "My son, I am a farmer as my father before me and his before him. It is all I've known and it's a good and honest life. I believe that I would be failing as your father if I did not give you the opportunity you deserve. The advanced folk can show you a way of life of which I couldn't dream… but I think it is your choice."

Taam sat dumbfounded. What should I do? I would miss my mother, my sister, and Father—not to mention my friends. On the other hand, what would my friends say? Why would it matter if I never see them again? I don't know! I don't know!

Loy stood up, pulled some coins from a small pouch, and laid them on the table. He stooped down to just above Taam's eye level. "You will be sixteen years of age in fifteen days. On that day, if you decide to take the challenge, be at the place you removed the dam at midday. Be there alone. While you ponder, drink a tea each morning from this herb." He handed Taam a small tin. He took up his staff, pulled his hood over his head, and exited into the dark street.

Hym and Taam sat for a moment, stunned by Loy's abruptness. As the barman came over to clear the table and collect the coins, they spoke of common events of the community and pleasantries and to the trader about his goods.

All the while Taam's mind was in a whirl of indecision. It was giving him a headache. So he decided to put the thoughts off until the morrow.

II

Manhood

The next morning Taam rose with the sun. As he opened the shutter, the rays seemed to poke him in the eyes. The events from the all important meeting yesterday were fuzzy in his mind, as if he were already forgetting it. He thought about all the things that had been said, the questions that had been asked, and the ones that hadn't.

He pulled the tin from his pocket and stared at it. It was round with embossed runes on top. The tin had been painted at one time, but the paint had rubbed off from miles of travel in a pack or pocket. Taam went to the fire and made a small cup of tea from the large kettle sitting by the dull embers.

Outside the cool air made him narrow his eyes. A shiver went down his spine as he took a sip of the hot beverage. Why did Loy ignore his question?

*Did I really mean i*t? thought Taam. *Was I just making jest when I spoke to the river?* He took another sip of the tea. It felt good going down, spreading a warm feeling throughout his body. His breath made smoke as he exhaled.

He doesn't know where I removed the dam. How will he know where to meet me? Should I try to find him? Do I even want to meet him there? What does he mean 'to achieve balance'?

Hym came out of the small house, taking a deep breath then exhaling audibly. "I'm going hunting today. Would you like to come? Maybe we'll even spook a deer."

Taam agreed and they decided to go after breakfast.

The day proceeded almost as if nothing out of the ordinary had happened. The next week, too, was completely uneventful.

Each morning Taam met the sun, had some tea, and pondered many things. He began coordinating his thoughts breaking them down into smaller ideas and addressing each one in order of importance. This, in fact, was new to him. He realized now why Loy had given him the tea—it must help the mind, he thought.

On the eighth day, Taam pulled up a stump from a bog and hewed it into a plow blade of his own design. It felt natural. To Taam's surprise his father was awestruck with the design and the craftsmanship. "This is my son, and he is gifted beyond me," he kept saying.

This embarrassed Taam but it also made him feel a pride he had never felt before.

The next day, his mother wept every time they met. "We're so proud of you," she said. "I'll miss you so much." Taam kept reminding her that he had yet not made his decision.

When the eleventh day had ended and the family had gone to bed, Taam lay awake, pondering and weighing the final question—the question he had decided should be the deciding factor. The question which, above all, he must answer without reserve. *If I leave, will the negative effect on my family be outweighed by the greater good of mankind? That makes me sound so much more important than I feel,* he thought. *I know the gifted ones are really wise, but what will I come to be, if I learn from them?* Then he heard something.

Taam rose and went to the front door. The voices of his mother and father were coming from outside. His mother was crying again, but he could still understand her. She was asking his father to tell him not to go.

"My dear, dear wife, please understand this one thing. A man wants to pass on a legacy to his namesake. My son, my namesake, would receive exactly the same thing I received when my father passed over: a small farm which, with hard work, will keep him and his family safe and reasonably comfortable until he passes over. In a hundred years, he would just be another farmer whom no one remembers. My great great-grandfather's name is only known by me—he was just a farmer. Taam has the gifts which could help him become someone not only of great importance, but someone who could make a difference in this land."

Taam returned to his bed. "I guess that answers that question," he muttered. He peered through the crack in the shutters, making out the outline of the leafless moonlit trees. A chill set in on his back so he pulled the cover up around his shoulders and tight to his neck, then drifted off to sleep.

On Taam's day of birth he rose to find everyone up before him. Hym passed in front of Taam's small room and seeing him awake he spoke. "Ah, some tea is in order. Pass me your tin, son."

Taam reached over and pulled the tin from the pocket of his cloak hanging by his bed, and tossed it overhand to his father. He rose, made his cot, and dressed. He reached behind his bed and pulled out the small package, which he had wedged there.

It was the custom that, on the day of birth each year, a child must present their mother with a gift, something made by their own hand. Taam had spent countless hours on this one. Over six months he had carved four figurines. Each one was an exact representation of a family member. They were carved from the whitest soapstone, and as they stood on a shelf, they could hold hands with all the others in any order they were placed. The detail was remarkable and made it obvious that a great deal of time had been spent on this gift.

Stepping into the larger common area, he saw his mother sitting at the table and his sister serving up an early breakfast of porridge and ham.

Hym handed Taam a mug of tea. "This day you formally become a man," he said, "even though you have acted as such for some time." The entire family turned and smiled at him.

"I am only what you have made me," said Taam, "and I wish only to honor you both. I know how important the family is to you, Mother. I present you with this small token, which pales in the love this family has for you."

His mother carefully took the package, holding it as if it might break. She looked into his eyes. "I love you too, my son," she said.

She slowly opened the wrapping, seeming to savor each second, and finally eased the first figure out. It was the one of Hym.

"Oh, Hym," she said as she delicately caressed the face of the figure. She raised it to her lips and gingerly kissed it. Setting Hym on the table, she eased out the next figure. It was of herself. She peered at it then reached up and touched her hair. "Taam, it's as if I were looking into a mirror." The next was his sister, and their mother looked at her daughter and said, "Sha, the love your brother has for you is evident."

The last figure was Taam. It had been the hardest one to make, as reflections were hard to come by and his mother had the only mirror the family owned. She pressed the figure against her bosom.

"Taam, I will look upon your likeness and know you're safe. Go into the world and have adventures. Find your place." She placed all four figurines in a circle on the table. The family encircled her, each one grasping the others in a group hug. Tears flowed from everyone's eyes.

III

Change

After the morning meal, Taam packed what he planned to take. His hunting knife, handed down from Grandfather, hung from his waist. A small pack would carry everything else easily, a change of clothes, a pair of gloves, the small carving kit. He also packed a palm-sized copper cauldron for cooking and a small tin mug his mother had given him. His father gave him a flint for starting fire.

Sha gave him a small stone she had found. It was the size of a fat plum, yet lens-shaped and clear with a bluish tint. Looking through it made objects appear larger. She told him that she thought if he polished it he might be able to see small splinters with it.

By midmorning he was packed and had given his other possessions to those whom he thought would benefit from them. Most Taam returned to his parents who had given them to him.

Saying their farewells seemed to drain the energy from everyone. Taam asked his father to pass on his farewells to his friends as they had not been told of the decision he had made. His father and he had discussed in depth what their reactions might be. They couldn't be allowed to sway Taam's conclusion. After the choice was made, they also decided not to say anything about Taam's gifts or the training he was about to undergo. If the clerics ever came to the settlement asking about the gifted ones, it would be best if no one was aware of goings on.

It was a fact that no one spoke of, but all knew, that the clerics were bent on destroying the gifted ones. They preached that the gods were responsible for all that happened and that they controlled fate. It was said the gifted ones were under the power of dark magic and would destroy the world by angering the gods. The clerics, and especially Mach—the most powerful cleric—were trying to convince the king, Han, to make it law to worship the gods and shun the gifted ones. But the gifted ones had been around for centuries before the clerics.

As midday approached, Taam set out for the place on the river where he'd removed the dam. He carried his bow and quiver, his pack and knife. The day was cool and clouds moved overhead swiftly toward the southeast. Most of the leaves were gone from the trees and they made crunching sounds beneath his feet.

Taam stopped where he could barely see his small house through the trees.

"Supple stone which hold features and love, my family," he said. "I beg you to reveal to my mother the truth of my journey, for she needs to know." Taam turned and trotted on.

As he approached the river, he could see Loy sitting on a fallen tree, a branch clustered with bright red berries in his hand. He was plucking the berries off, squeezing them, making them pop, and then rolling the seeds around in his fingers until the clear flesh was off them. He piled the seeds onto a cloth in his lap. His little camp was precisely where the dam had been.

"Teacher," said Taam, "how did you know where I removed the dam?"

Loy continued retrieving the seeds for a while before answering. "The Mother told me."

"My mother?" asked Taam.

"No, *the* Mother," said Loy. "Do you have my tin?"

Taam pulled the little tin from his pocket and handed it to Loy. What does he mean, the Mother? he thought. No one was here but my father and me. We never told anyone where it was. Who is the Mother? "Who do you mean?" he asked.

Loy stopped and looked at him. "You speak to her all the time. You just asked her to keep your mother informed. Why would you ask a stranger to keep your mother informed? Would you not ask your closest friend, or perhaps a family member?"

Taam was so surprised he didn't know what to say. No one could know what he'd asked the stone figurines to do. He didn't even know himself what he'd actually asked. Hearing it from Loy made him think about what he'd done. *What would the figures do if I'm injured? What would happen if I died?* His mother would know the truth, but how?

Loy went back to his task and began again. "Taam, our Mother, this place where we live, the earth, the wind, the water, the stones, the animals, everything, including ourselves—we are all one. Like a family, we are. We suckle from Her teat. We share the strengths of our brothers and sisters. Our Mother teaches us, nourishes us, and provides everything we need for life. Of course it's up to us to make the right choices in life. She will let us make our own decisions, but She will also require us to take responsibility for those choices. When we make good choices, She rewards us. When we make bad choices, we suffer the fate of those choices. Therefore, we make the fate we endure. We also effect others' fate in the same way."

The task was done, and Loy bundled up the small pack of seeds and slipped them into his pack. He pointed at a small knee-high plant at the edge of the camp. From a rosette at the ground rose long, wavy, dark green leaves, which drooped at the ends.

"Pull that up and take the root," said Loy.

Taam did as he was told. The root was fat and oblong and Taam chopped off the leaves and slipped the root in his pack.

"Don't do it after the first snow," said Loy. After gathering the rest of his own pack, Loy and Taam began their journey westward.

As mid-afternoon came upon the two, the sky began to darken and a bitter wind cut at them. They leaned to the right against the wind as they passed through a grassy meadow. Taam knew it was going to get very cold during the night.

Loy turned right on a well-worn path. A half hour of battling wind in the face made Taam think. If Loy was so in tuned to the Mother, then why did he battle nature? *Why doesn't he get the Mother to ease up on the wind? Mother should protect us, shouldn't She? We shouldn't have left knowing a storm was on the way.*

15

The path wound through some evergreen trees, then opened out onto a small hilltop. A stone structure sat in the middle of the clearing. The walls were four times the height of a man and curved as if the building bulged. The corners were rounded and Taam noticed there were no straight lines anywhere. The color of the stone gradually faded from gray close to the ground to white at the top. It was larger than any house Taam had seen and there were no windows.

As they approached a massive wooden door, Taam relaxed his grip on the traveling cloak—it felt good when the building blocked the wind. Loy grasped the latch and pulled the door open.

Is this Loy's house? thought Taam.

As he walked in, the warmth seemed to remove the chill

he'd been feeling completely. As Taam turned and pushed the door closed, huge rain drops began to fall. He heard Loy say, "Thank you, Mother."

The entrance was of dark gray stone. The floor and the walls were all the same, with no differentiation between the floor and walls and ceiling. Six sconces holding torches were evenly spaced around the small room, with one on each side of the single opening. Moving through the opening they moved down a hallway, which followed the outer wall of the building. The corridor was two cubits in breadth and five cubits high. It wound around the entire structure several times, moving downward ever steeper until it opened into a large circular room.

Loy stopped and snuffed the torch in the indention wrought into the wall sconce. He placed the dead torch in the sconce then proceeded into the room. Around the walls were shelves packed with scrolls and bound books. There were highly polished tables and chairs placed around the room. In the center was a spiral stairway, which circled upward through the ceiling and continued downward through the floor. The ceiling seamed to glow—but no torches, candles, or chandeliers were present. The glow was bright enough to read by.

Loy turned to Taam. "This is the library. You'll be here a lot this winter."

"Do you live here?" asked Taam.

Loy looked at him for a moment. "You will address me as 'Teacher' from now on. You will show respect to all living things, and respect will be earned by you." He paused for another long moment. "We will be staying here for a while." He turned and walked to the stair. Taam followed.

As they descended, light was not required, as the ceiling in the stairwell glowed like the one in the library. It was too high to touch and Taam almost stumbled as he gazed at it. He thought Loy must have heard him trip, because his teacher spoke.

"Do not fall, as it may injure both of us. Taam, I will answer all your questions in due time."

Taam grasped the rail and continued, thinking, *Well I've got lots of them.*

After seven full turns they arrived at the bottom. Taam's chin fell to his chest, as he had never imagined anything like this.

IV

First Lesson

There before them stretched a vast room, larger across than the entire structure above. The ceiling glowed as if the sun was shining through velum. The floor and distant walls were white. The room itself was a grand sight, but what dominated Taam's attention was thirty cubits in front of them.

A bright sphere the size of a cantaloupe floated at about the height of a man and a half above the floor. Around it, circling it, were several other spheres. They weren't shining, but were different colors: red, tan, a blue and green one, one with a bladelike ring around it. Around some of them circled yet more spheres. They all moved at different speeds, but all seemed perfectly synchronized.

"This is a depiction of our Mother's physical self," said Loy. "But some feel that this is only Her fingertip."

They walked to the representation and Taam slowly circled it. He looked at each sphere intently, watching the path it took. He waved his hand over one of the balls as it passed, trying to detect any strings invisible to the eye, but there were none. He could see no physical force keeping it all in the air.

"We live on one of those orbs. Can you tell me which one?"

Taam looked at Loy puzzled. "We live on one of these?"

Loy smiled. "Yes, most people can't see beyond the horizon. They even think they could fall off the edge of the world. So let me show you." He pointed to the shining globe in the center. "This is Sol Solis. It is a powerful mass of energy. These orbs circling Sol Solis are worlds. The orbs circling them are moons— we call them lunas. Each time a world circles Sol Solis, a year is counted. Each time a luna circles a world, it is a month. Each time a world makes a complete revolution, it is a day and a night. Now, with that information, which one is the world we live on?"

Taam began by ruling out the worlds with more than one moon or ones with no moons at all. Then he pondered the colors. The vivid blue planet with the large green patch on it made him think. *The trees are all green and no other world even has green on it.*

He pointed to the blue-green world. "This one?" he asked.

"Why do you pick this one?" said Loy.

"Because it looks alive, but is the sea so large?"

"You have picked wisely. This is Mundus Terra. I don't know if those other worlds are alive or not. I suspect they must be because of all the power which is here. Even some lunas may abound with life. This is Mundus Rufus, the red world. Anyone can see it in the night sky." Loy named each world and Taam repeated them in an effort to remember.

"I want you to see the balance in it all," said Loy. "Each world circles Sol Solis and receives its power from it. And as each world circles it, the world spins, allowing the light and energy to evenly cover each world—creating the night and the day. We must have both to have balance. Each thing has an effect on another thing, and then another, and so on. The only way to prevent chaos is to maintain balance in all things."

Taam looked at Loy with questioning eyes. "Teacher, is that what the advanced ones do, prevent chaos?"

The teacher smiled. "Not exactly, yet perhaps. All people must try to obtain balance in their lives. Few accomplish it, but balance allows one to understand their surroundings, live in harmony with them, find happiness within them, and feel contentment by being a productive part of it all. Your father is a farmer and is in harmony with the soil he tills. He takes care of the soil and it, in turn, takes care of him. Your environment is much more." He pointed at the orbs floating around the Sol Solis.

"Come Taam, it is time to rest." He took the boy to the other side of the stairwell, where there was a structure with open arched doorways and windows speckling the white walls. As Loy walked Taam to the perimeter wall, he pointed out runes within the arches. He explained that the old language was etched on the tops of the arches, describing the use of each room. "As you will learn the language, you will be allowed to use the room it describes."

They stopped at a doorway. "This is your sleeping room. You will call it 'cubiculum.'" Loy pointed at the runes at the top of the archway.

Taam repeated, "Cubiculum" and inside the room a bed, a table, and a chair appeared. "Each room will do the same as you correctly speak its name," said Loy.

They walked to the next doorway and Loy said, "Lavatio." The interior of the room seemed to fade into focus, with a large basin in the floor. A small stream of water flowed out of a plain spigot protruding from the wall. Another basin of water sat upon a white stone table, with a soft hand cloth on a hook above it. A chamber pot sat in a corner, away from the rest of the plain furnishings.

"This room is for washing," said Loy. "Use this room every day. Do you have the root I asked you to bring?"

Taam thrust his hand into his pack and pulled it out. Loy took the root and cut it into slabs the thickness of his finger. "Use this as an alternative for potash soap," he said. He turned and left Taam standing. About four doors down the hallway, he said, "Cubiculum," then walked in.

Taam went back to his room and tried to enter. A force seemed to hold him at bay. He stepped back and said, "Cubiculum," and then stepped through the door. The room was compact and plain. He placed his pack on the table and began unpacking. With each item he removed, he wondered how these insignificant things would assist him in maintaining balance in the entire world. If what he had seen this day was not a trick, then it might be possible to learn what he needed to change the world.

So much information in so little time and so much magic, he thought, and I'm right in the heart of it. I don't know what's real and what isn't. Even this room seemed to appear from thin air. What does tomorrow hold?

He looked around for a place to put the clear stone Sha gave him. Looking at the wall, he quietly said to himself, "I need a shelf right there." Slowly an indention formed in the wall, just large enough for the stone. He gingerly placed it on the newly formed shelf, and smiling, he completed his unpacking and went to bathe.

The warm bath relaxed him and hunger began to gnaw at his stomach. Back in his room, he ate a piece of bread his mother had slipped into his pack for the trip. Lying back on the bed, he stared up at the blank white ceiling, thinking of the day's events. As images danced through his mind, his thoughts began to slow until sleep overtook his weariness.

V

Balance

Taam awoke slowly and began to look around. It took a moment to remember where he was. This was the first time he had slept overnight in a place which was not his home. Without exterior windows, there was no way of knowing what time it was—and that was unsettling. He rose and dressed, then leaned out the door looking for Loy.

He walked to the stairwell and then to the floating orbs. He wondered how they all stayed in such perfect harmonious movement. They each spun at different rates, but the movements seemed perfect in every way. Taam reached out and touched the nearest world, just to see if it were real. As it grazed the tip of his finger it began to wobble slightly but kept on its orbit. Taam watched its orbit expand until the orb spun out of control, striking another orb, and on until all of the display had flung apart and dissolved into nothing. Taam stared at the empty space with his chin on his chest.

From behind him Loy's voice broke the silence. "It became out of balance."

The surprised student spun around to see his teacher sitting on the stairwell steps, drinking a mug of something hot. Taam couldn't say anything—words just wouldn't come.

Loy reached up to a higher step, picked up a second mug, and held it out to Taam. "Have some tea."

Taam thought it odd that his teacher wasn't angry at his action, but quickly accepted the fact. He followed Loy upstairs, past the library, to the roof. As they came to the landing, a heavy timber door stood before them. When Loy grasped the handle the ceiling's glow quickly dimmed to darkness. The door swung inwards and the cold rushed in with it. There was ice and snow on the rooftop and even though it was very cloudy, Taam could tell it was early morning.

Loy told him he liked to come up and see Sol Solis in the morning; it helped him feel in step with it. Taam felt the same but he said nothing. At the wall he could see the clearing around the structure. It was easy to see that the large room was well below ground and extended out to the tree line.

Snow covered the ground and the many trees had lost their last remaining leaves in a storm during the night. The wind still blew and the cold cut through his light tunic. The warm tea felt good cupped in both hands, and even better warming his inside.

After a short while, Loy turned and Taam followed him inside. The light brightened as the door closed. As they approached the library Taam asked what the word to breakfast was.

Loy agreed it would be a nice word to know, smiling at his young student. They stopped in the library and retrieved a couple of scrolls then went downstairs.

Loy taught him 'ceno' to access the dining room, which had several stone tables and benches. It could serve at least a hundred people, possibly more. One table, set for two, had bowls of fruit, breakfast cakes, honey, and a hot kettle of tea. The utensils, bowls, kettle, and other dishes were all made of the same white stone as everything else.

As the two sat down to dine, Taam asked, "Why does everything look the same? Everything is made of this white stone and there is no color."

"In this place things are as we see them in our mind," explained Loy. "Since you had no idea what to expect when you got here, everything is in its simplest form. This place was made to teach. It has power built into it to assist in doing just that. When this place has several students within it, several minds come up with new innovative ways of seeing the world. All the students profit from it. As I've said before, I'm a teacher, but I am also a student. You are a student, but you also are a teacher. The experiences you have had in your sixteen years will reflect onto other people, and you'll learn from others. That is the essence of life: balance."

The conversation paused as Loy poured fresh mugs of tea.

"Look at this bowl, what do you see?"

Taam stared at the bowl, wondering what Loy wanted him to say. "I see a bowl."

"Right," said Loy, "now see it as a pitcher of cold milk. Visualize it in your mind, making the form change, and don't forget the milk."

Taam stared at the bowl, letting his eyes go out of focus. A picture of his mother's pitcher with cold buttermilk in it was firmly implanted in his mind. When he focused back on the dish, the bowl slowly shifted its shape into the bright yellow decanter he was familiar with. As Taam looked at it wide-eyed, Loy poured two cups of buttermilk. When his teacher sat the pitcher on the table, the yellow color seemed to flow into the tabletop, into the rest of the utensils and dishes.

"You might want to try the buttermilk before you turn it yellow," said Loy.

"How did I do this thing, Teacher?" asked Taam.

"All in time, in due time," said Loy.

"Teacher, will there be other students here?"

Loy explained that many teachers were retrieving students at all times. "A student stays with the first teacher for a while, and then with the next, and so on. The two travel the world and stay different places. There are several ludusa, or schools. This is Arborludusium, or 'school of the trees.' There may be over a hundred students here at any time. We are here for the library. There are some important things you must learn very quickly."

Loy explained the need to speak and understand the old language. "It is descriptive in exactness, and the meanings of the words do not change with time or region. The teachings of the medical uses of plants are stored in this library. The school is the perfect place to learn how to manipulate the power of the world, especially for one who has not been raised in the skill."

"You mean people are around this magic when they are children?" asked Taam.

"There is that word again, 'magic'. Children can be raised by teachers just as they can be raised by farmers," said Loy.

Taam looked down at the table, thinking, I must learn to express myself differently. This teacher seems to view things with such exactness.

With that Loy rose from the table, picked up the scrolls, and said, "Let us begin."

The classes that day were mostly on the old language, and by the end of the day Taam was able to enter three more rooms. One of them contained some very interesting games. Loy showed him one called chess. In the old language, the game was called 'scaccarium.' It had extravagantly carved pieces and a board to play on. It was a war game requiring two players, who commanded their armies. It took a while to remember how each piece moved. Taam liked the Equester or cavalry the most.

The rooms began to change as Taam learned. Scrollwork began appearing in places, which had been in need of some character. The faces of chess pieces began showing up artistically carved in walls and over doors. Over the next several weeks, Taam learned to read and write enough words and phrases to access most of the rooms.

Every morning Taam and his teacher met the sun, and watched it set in the evening. They would breakfast and then class would commence. On breaks they would walk and talk or play chess. Each time they dined Loy asked questions about how Taam would react in different scenarios.

Taam spent countless hours in the library. It was a warm place and it didn't echo. The echoes seemed to go on forever in his mind. It made him feel small and he wasn't use to that. At home the house didn't echo. It felt close and warm, like a hug. He missed his family.

The old language soon seemed to be drilled into his brain. Sometimes Taam would even think in the old language. When he did, things around him would react to his very thoughts.

One time, he caught himself reading a scroll as he walked from the shelf toward the tables without thinking. The chair moved by itself and, as he sat down, gently slipped under him. Taam stopped reading and jumped up as if someone were with him, but he was alone. His thoughts seemed to make things happen without him consciously wanting them to. This was strange to him and even frightened him a little. He decided he would ask Loy about this.

As they sat for their meal later in that day, Taam asked, "Teacher, the Arborludusium is a very powerful place. The chair in the library moved for me when I sat. I didn't think it to move, it just moved. What does this mean?"

Loy answered in a concerned voice. "Were you thinking in the old language?"

"I think maybe, yes," replied Taam. "I was reading a scroll on the travels of a farmer named Cain. I just sat on the chair and it moved under me as if someone assisted it."

"That's interesting," said Loy. "Usually it takes months for this to occur. The ludusa magnifies your abilities to help you learn both how to control power and to use good judgment. When you speak in the old language, it will respond in this way. When you think in the old language, the ludusa will only provide the raw materials. You must be aware of your every thought—although it is usually spoken, for some people a thought in the old language is just as powerful. You must also remember: if you react this quickly to your training, your abilities outside will be evident to others. You must learn the judgment which must be used with this ability. People don't normally understand what we do or how we do it."

VI

Cold Feet

After the meal they left the building. "Can we go outside?" asked Taam.

"I think that would be a great idea," answered his teacher.

It was clear and cool and the ground crunched beneath their feet .The still air was full of the sounds of nature and seemed deafening to Taam. It felt good to be outside. The twice daily visits to the roof were nice, but this… *this* was like being set free. He ran down the path with his arms outstretched, breathing in the wonderful smells of the woods.

But there was a sound, a sudden feeling of danger. He stopped, listening intently. He looked back at Loy, who looking to his right. He motioned to Taam to come back to him. Taam was at the edge of the clearing and Loy was about halfway across it. The student moved toward his teacher, thinking "Leviter" over and over, making him lighter on his feet, allowing him to move silently.

As he approached Loy, Taam noticed Loy was looking up at him. Taam had risen a knee's height off the ground. When he realized, he stopped repeating the word in his mind and crashed down at Loy's feet. He looked up at his teacher, expecting a response of disapproval. But Loy was looking back in the direction from which the sound had originated. Both stood quietly, watching and listening.

For a long while nothing unusual occurred. Then a breeze rustled the few leaves on the ground under the trees. The boughs began to rub together with a creaking sound. And the sound was getting closer.

Then loose leaves stirred, starting in the trees and moving into the clearing, straight toward the two. The leaves whirled around, rising to the height of the treetops at the edge of the clearing, then gently floating down as the spinning air mass moved on.

Taam became uneasy and took a step backwards. His teacher watched intently as the small whirling breeze came closer. When it reached Loy, he reached out and caught a green leaf—the movement was gone, allowing all the dry, dead leaves to float gently to the ground.

"We have a communication," he said.

"Teacher, what was that?" asked Taam.

"A Procella, or tempest, charged with a task," said the now smiling Loy. "This is a note from a friend. Let us go back inside and see what it says." He turned and began walking toward the school. "Don't concentrate so hard without being aware of what you are doing. If someone saw you in a town, well, they would feel only fear. Fear upsets balance. Their fear will strike out at you and others like you."

"It wasn't much of a trip outside," said Taam with his feelings obviously hurt.

"Well go. There is a small stream over there." Loy pointed off into the woods. "It is a very relaxing place. Just be back in before Sol Solis has retired for the evening."

With that Taam was off and running for the woods with a grin on his face and a song in his heart.

He spent a few hours at the small brook, listening to the birds and watching the fish in the clear, cold water. The sound of the water, the smell of mud and moss, and the feel of the cold made him feel alive again. The grind of learning to read and write an entirely new language and learn the names of plants he had only seen in the scrolls was overwhelming. The school was so confining, too. When he'd first arrived it had seemed so large, but now the walls seemed to close in around him. The mornings and evenings on the roof were alright, but this place made him feel so free.

He took his boots off and placed his feet in the water until the aching of the cold stopped and his feet went numb. Upon deciding to head back, he found it was hard to walk with his feet so cold, and as the numbness began to subside, the aching returned. Oh the pain, the sweet, sweet pain—it brought the reality of his new life back crashing down upon his shoulders.

The words, the writing, the balance what good is it?

He stopped in his tracks with a realization. *What have I been studying for if I can't use it in real life?* Taam looked down at his feet and stretched out his hand with his palm open. He spoke the words in the old language to ease the pain. It was gone.

"Now *that* is magic," he said, and off he ran, feeling as though he could cure the world of all its ills.

During the evening meal Loy told him that the message they had received was from another teacher who would be coming soon. This teacher would be training Taam in different courses than Loy was teaching. He wouldn't tell Taam what the courses were to be. That will be up to Master Vele.

So then Taam told Loy what he had done in the woods.

"Taam," frowned Loy, "what if you had spoken a word wrong? What if the meaning wasn't what you wanted? You might have lost your feet completely! You need to learn much more before you inflict yourself with the possibility of errors."

"But Teacher, I didn't—"

Before he could finish, Loy held up a hand. "In the morning we shall step up your training, as time is now short. Let us retire for the evening."

That night, Taam changed his room, making it appear as if he were in the woods by the brook. The water flowed by his bed and the stars were bright in the sky above. The furniture appeared as though trees had grown up in the shape of each piece. Even the little shelves were now in little knot holes.

Taam went to sleep smiling.

VII

Magic Class

"There are several types of what one might call magic," said Loy. "The most common is known as 'hand of deception.' This is used by performers to make things appear as they are not." Loy held up his left hand with his palm facing him. He appeared to pull his thumb with his right hand, extending it past his fingertips then replacing it. "This takes no special powers or gifts, just a specific knowledge and a clever hand." Taam thought that that was an interesting trick he would show Sha one day.

"The next type is known as 'oro vis vires,'" Loy continued, "which means, 'to speak power.' You state your request, and the energy around you performs the task. If you know exactly how or what to say, you can get a very accurate result. This you did when you asked the river to share her bounty—you received fish. What you didn't understand is that a lot more was said. The river gave you four fish. Do you know why?"

Taam thought for a moment. "Was it because there were four in my family?"

"Yes," said Loy. "The river knew this and shared her bounty with your entire family. When you refer to yourself, you also refer to your lineage. That is why it is important to make clear what you speak, or even what you think." Loy leaned up, pulled one knee to his chest, easing the heel of his foot onto the seat with him. "Most people use the vetus lingua, or old language to oro vis vires, because the meanings of words in common languages tend to change over time. The old language, when properly used, is very specific.

"Another form of magic is that called by action. This is an old method lost to many and used by persons unable to express themselves in other ways. The magic is there all around us—most people could use it if they had an understanding. Some people see it, but don't believe it. This tale should help you understand:

"There once was a woodsman and his boy. They went into the woods, as they do, and the woodsman chose a fine tree to take. He didn't know it had been struck by the fire from above. As he cut the tree, a bough broke loose and fell upon him. It pinned him down, as it was an old tree and the bough was heavy. The boy was small and young, yet he lifted the bough off his father and allowed him to escape death. The woodsman himself could not lift the bough, but his son did. This was magic empowered by an act. They did not know this, and afterward the boy tried to lift the bough time and time again, yet could never do it."

"Teacher did this truly happen?" asked Taam.

Loy looked at him. He set his foot down firmly. "Taam, I will never speak an untruth to anyone and I will never jest while in a lesson."

Taam looked down remorsefully.

Loy went on. "Another kind of magic is that for which I know no name. I have not seen it myself. Some have told of persons who have the ability to change their form. It may well be possible, but I'd think that, without the proper training, one might change into something he would later regret— or possibly change into something and be unable to change back. I would hate to change into a plant only to be eaten by a deer."

Taam smiled. "Or a snowflake only to melt in the spring." They both smiled.

Loy became very solemn. "The magic of darkness is also strong. It lives without light. People call out to what they call spirits, but it is another type of oro vis vires. This magic is the opposite of everything good. It is used to manipulate others. It feeds on the energy within the person using it. It contaminates everything and everyone it touches. Sickness and death surround it. It cannot be obliterated, because it is spawned by the lack of everything. It is in theory not magic, but a lack of magic. In a more precise statement, it is not the manipulation of power, it is the expenditure of power." He paused for a while. "The ones who use this are called 'veneficus.' You will know who they are when you see them.

"The magic that I will teach you, if you really want to call it that, is of energy. It is the life force of the stars, the sky, the sea, the soil, the very thing which binds us together. It is pure and never ending. The sun, Sol Solis, is a powerful energy. Its energy showers on to Mundus Terra and heats us. That energy now resides in us. When we use our energy to lift a stone, the energy resides in the stone. If we drop the stone, the energy then resides in the soil the stone struck. It never truly ceases to exist. We then take this energy and employ it in constructive ways. It is what made the world and it wants to be constructive. It needs only to be set into motion.

"Heat is the easiest type energy to manipulate." Loy reached behind him and picked up three small bundles of twigs. He leaned forward onto one knee and made three small stacks spaced about a pace apart. "Take your hands and rub them together to create heat." They both briskly rubbed their hands together in front of them. "And then," said Loy as he quickly thrust his hands away from him toward one of the piles, "Ignis!" The pile suddenly caught and began to burn.

Taam then thrust his hand away from him with his palms facing another small pile and yelled "*Ignis!*" Flames stretched out from his palms, blasting the pile in every direction. Taam closed his fists tight with utter surprise on his face. The soil in front of him had flames leaping waist high. The heat was intense.

Loy, expressionless, held out one open hand and slowly lowered it, speaking the word meaning 'extinguish,' in the old language. As he did, the flame lessened until it was extinguished. He looked at Taam. "I said heat was the easiest energy to manipulate—heat is part of the fire."

Taam couldn't believe what had just happened. *I made fire, immense fire.* How many times had there been no flint? How many times had the kindling been wet? *What would Father say? Father. I wonder what he is doing right now. I made fire!*

Loy's eyes had no excitement in them—it was as if he wasn't surprised at all.

But his father had been so proud of him. It used to embarrass him sometimes, but now he missed it: the pat on the back, the pride his father had. It had made him feel uncomfortable, kind of young, and maybe even childish. *Grow up,* he thought to himself, *you're a man now.* He directed his attention back to Loy.

"Now think of what you are going to do before you act. See each step of your action in your mind, and see the reaction to what you do before it occurs. Try it again."

Taam stared at the last pile of twigs thinking, *Alright, I'm going to rub my hands together, push the heat into the twigs and say, "Ignis."* He pictured the bundle burning in his mind.

Suddenly the pile began to smoke, then flames began to consume it. He looked at Loy, wide-eyed. "I didn't do anything!"

Loy grinned. "Oh, but you did. You methodically stated what you wanted to happen, included *how* it was to happen, and with one word—in your mind—directed the power to ignite the twigs."

Taam stared into the flames, still sorting out his thoughts.

"In all things balance…" continued Loy. "You must answer all the questions that may be asked when you manipulate the power our Mother holds. Who, what, where, why, when, and how must all be known. If you relieve the pain in your feet and do not consider all the questions that may be asked, you could lose all feeling in them forever. Do you understand?"

Taam nodded. He stretched out his hand, lowering the fire until it withered away to cool coals. "Does the Arborludusium enhance what I just did?" asked Taam.

"The school does help in certain ways, but what you just accomplished was all you. It only supplied us with the tinder. With all you have learned in the short time you have been here, you have shown a great talent. It is obvious you will be able to accomplish a great deal in your lifetime."

Taam appreciated the complement and it made all the hard work seem worthwhile. With his spirit uplifted, they began again with different ways of performing simple tasks. Shielding and deflecting projectiles was interesting. The projectile would approach and then slow down until it stopped a palm's width from the body, or the path of flight would arc around the body. Within a few hours Taam was able to lift large objects, including liquids, cause sand to form into glass shapes, shape stones into small statues, and make a small gust of air move across the room. All thought was in the old language and he pictured each action in his mind before it happened.

"We have much more to learn," Loy explained. "Most importantly the thought process must be in the old language with his whole heart and mind."

"It is getting easier to think in the old language, Teacher," said Taam.

"Good, because when Master Vele arrives, your work will double," said Loy without letting Taam see his face.

I think he takes his teaching too seriously, thought Taam. I hope this Master Vele isn't as rigid as Loy.

VIII

Master Vele

Within a week the decorating scheme of Taam's quarters had stretched across the entire school. The colors and sounds of the forest were everywhere. The ceiling was an endless blue sky in the day and a star filled moonlit sky at night. Squirrels ran and played and leapt from tree to tree. Song birds sang to the trees and there was no echo.

"This is a comfortable setting to learn in," said Loy with a wink. "I should have sent you to the brook earlier."

Taam noticed that his teacher smiled more since the change in decor. They would sit on some logs near the small stream for their class time and draw runes in the sand. They spoke of ethics, medicine, and the old language.

One day Loy taught him how to summon a procella and give it a task. Creating the swirling tempest was much harder than just making the wind blow. Choosing a task for it to follow was not a challenge for Taam, he knew exactly to ask. Taam used the old language to have it carry him across the school grounds and then back again. The little spiraling pool of wind snatched him from the floor and whipped across the huge room with the dazed student spinning round and round. It moved him so fast that he couldn't focus his thoughts, yet it seemed to take forever and he just wanted it to stop. The language was lost to him.

Upon arriving at the spot he had requested, the procella promptly dropped him and disappeared into still air. Taam's head was still spinning as he turned a full turn, dropped to his hip being unable to stand. He tried to hold himself up but the spinning pulled him the rest of the way down. His face planted flat on the floor. Dry heaving from the nauseating ride, tears came to his eyes as he wretched. The whole world seemed to spin around him.

Loy grabbed his sides and fell off his log laughing. Eventually Taam recovered from the dizzy condition, pulled himself up, and staggered back to the log where Loy was still drying his eyes. Taam felt cold a clammy and his stomach was still queasy.

His grinning teacher handed him a cup of water. "That wasn't quite thought out, was it?"

"There has to be a way to make that work," Taam replied.

"You're not the first to try that, and I dare say you'll probably try it again. Just don't send yourself too far, as you may not make it alive," said Loy.

A distant sound of snickering grabbed their attention. Turning toward the stairway in the center of the school, they saw the source. Three ladies stood on the stairs, and they obviously had seen the entire debacle. The two younger ladies weren't much older than Taam and were clearly identical twins. Their black hair had slight curls and framed their faces perfectly. Their eyes were light crystal blue and full of life. They stood tall, dressed in warm woolen robes with the hoods pulled back.

The other lady had pulled off her traveling robe and draped it over one arm. Her smock was green and tight fitting. Her hair was dull amber and her face was hard. Lines ran from her high cheek bones to the bottom of her jaw. Even with a smile on her face she held an air of authority.

Loy and Taam rose from their places. "Master Vele!" said Loy with excitement in his tone. He bowed low and Taam followed suit.

"I thought you said you had a new student," exclaimed Vele in a deeper voice than Taam expected. "This one is at a level higher than you led me to believe."

Loy pulled himself up. "You honor me and my student with compliments. Please come and let us honor you with a warm meal and a game of chess."

Master Vele smiled and, with the two young women, strode into the grassy courtyard toward them. "These girls are my wards and my students. This is Melane and this is Delane and they make me proud daily," said Master Vele.

"This is Taam," said Loy, "and he surprises me regularly." With the introductions over, they went to have the midday meal.

"Master," said Melane. "Look at the squirrels playing, isn't it beautiful?"

Master Vele explained to them about the school, the method by which the power was amplified, and the limits of those powers. "This is Arborludusium or school of the trees," she told them.

The girls seemed to be intrigued by this and looked at each other, smiling as if they could read each other's mischievous thoughts. Taam knew the look well from his sister. *If those two are anything like Sha and half as sneaky, only harsh things will come from this.* he thought. As the five entered the room, small white flowers popped up all along the path they had just walked.

The meal was interesting, with Master Vele and Loy speaking of times when the school had bulging seams from the number of students and teachers. Loy told of the time one of the students melted the main stairwell into a pool of lava, and Master Vele remembered when one student had made everyone look identical to him. This had really angered his female classmates and they'd made him wear an itchy sackcloth frock for a month after that. They spoke of teachers that they knew, and of where they were, and of some who were gone forever. When the conversation leaned toward lost friends the twins changed the subject by giggling about Taam spinning across the courtyard. This brought a round of laughter and Taam felt red-faced.

He turned to Master Vele. "Master Vele, what do you teach?"

The table fell silent and the teacher studied Taam's eyes and face for a moment before answering. Taam made a point of looking directly at her eyes with sincerity and without blinking. Her face was contoured with lines of wisdom and though she looked fierce as a warrior, her eyes had a depth that he couldn't describe. His heart beat faster as the moment lasted for a full minute. Her lack of reply set him on edge.

"My name is of the old language, boy," she finally replied. "Do you know what it means?"

"Yes," he said. "It means soldier with light armor. Does that mean you teach one to fight?"

"No," she said, "I teach one *how* to fight. I also teach strategy, survival, physical strength, and *patience*."

She had not blinked the entire time they spoke and Taam now felt he might have overstepped his bounds—it seemed she had emphasized the word 'patience'.

Taam finally blinked and looked down. "With all respect, Master, I've been alone with my teacher for some time, and you seem so interesting."

She looked at Loy and smiled, showing her teeth. "Loy can be a little dry, but I can see by your lovely décor that you've overcome. Would you kindly show me around?"

When Taam looked up, he saw she was still looking at him, waiting for a reply. "I would be honored to show you around."

Since the meal was complete, they rose and followed Taam out. He described his woods and the words he used to create the trees and the representations of animals. "The pretty white flowers aren't mine," he said, smiling at the twins.

The day proceeded at a relaxing pace with a few games of chess, during which no one could get past six moves with Master Vele. The twins shed their traveling robes and sparred in the clear area near the stairs. Their grace and coordination were breathtaking, and Taam couldn't believe their speed. They were able to leap high enough to strike a tall man in the face with their foot extended straight out from the body. He thought to himself, *those two girls are able to do things I could only do with magic. If I could do that, well, I just hope the Master will teach me those moves.*

XI

Touched

Hym walked in to find his wife sitting at the table, holding the figurine of her son and weeping. She looked at her husband and smiled, reaching out to him. He moved over in an attempt to comfort her, placing his huge callused hand on her shoulder in a half hug, half leaning posture.

"He smiled at me today," she said.

Hym looked down at her, puzzled. "What?"

She looked up into her husband's eyes, holding up the carved figure, and repeated, "He smiled today."

The farmer looked over at the door of what used to be his son's room and pulled his wife closer, allowing her to bury her wet face in his waist. He patted her on the back.

When her tears were dry and the two were continuing the normal activities of their day, she spoke to her husband in depth about what she'd observed.

"My Love," she said. "I see things in the figurines during the day."

Hym started to speak but she gently placed her fingers on his lips to quiet him.

"They smile, they cry, they show love in their eyes. Their postures change. Even when you are in the field clearing the stump you've been working on, I can tell when you became thirsty."

She picked up her own likeness and looked into its face. "It shows me how I truly feel, even when I try hiding my feelings."

The two sat at the table across from each other and reached out, holding hands.

"Are you sure you are seeing what you think you are seeing?" asked Hym.

"Yes, and I believe Taam has bestowed this gift upon me so I would be comforted while he is gone," she replied.

"But what kind of magic is this?" said the farmer. "This could be thought of as evil if the wrong people knew of it. Maybe we should destroy the figurines."

"No," she said clutching the figure of her son close to her bosom. "You must make a cabinet for our little family. I will make a curtain to cover the front, so as not to be distracted when we have visitors. I am the only one who can see. I've tested Sha and I know she does not see it. No one knows but you, and we will keep it that way."

Hym agreed since he knew it would be a waste of time to do otherwise.

He spent the next day foraging through the storage for the materials to create a cabinet, which would honor the beauty of the perfectly carved figures his son had made. He chose each piece of wood, looking down it to see if it was bowed, then flexing it in his powerful hands to see if it was strong. He looked at the grain and pictured in his mind how it would look when finished and oiled. Having spent most of an hour in the quest for the perfect materials, he finally stopped and thought about his son. But his wife said Taam's figurine had smiled—he must be happy if he'd smiled. He wondered if Taam thought of his family much and where he was. "I certainly miss him," he whispered to himself.

"I miss him, too," said a voice behind him.

The farmer, startled, spun around to see Sha standing there. "You gave me a start, girl," he said. He took a couple of steps forward and hugged her. "Yes, my love, I miss him. It's a good thing you're here to keep me company." Tucking the bundle of building materials under one arm, he took his daughter in the other, and they walked to the tool shed.

During the evening meal, they talked about what the cabinet would look like. Hym wanted to oil the wood to a dark color so it would shine and stand out in the house. His wife, on the other hand, wanted it to be whitewashed so as not to be the centerpiece in the room. "The windows are what I want company to see. The view is perfect, and Taam's gift is for the family, not friends," she said.

The farmer and Sha agreed. They sat silently while they ate. When Hym had excused himself and went outside, Sha stared at her mother as if to say something but the words didn't seem to come. Noticing her daughter's troubled expression, she asked what was on her mind. With a mothers warm encouraging smile, Sha finally began to speak.

"Mother, I've been having dreams. I know this is normal, but the dreams that I'm talking about are happening while I'm awake."

"Do you mean daydreams, dear?" asked her mother, with a little concern in her voice.

"No mother, I know what daydreams are. These dreams are of things that wouldn't normally happen. They're more like visions," Sha said. "Once I saw Taam sitting with another man— Taam thrust out his hands and fire shot from them."

Her mother glanced casually at the set of figurines on the shelf across the room, then back to her daughter. "Listen Sha, your brother may well be one of the gifted ones, but there are limits on what people are capable of doing. Making fire come out of your hands just isn't possible. Not even for a gifted one," shaking her head as she spoke.

"Well, what *can* the gifted ones do, Mother?" asked Sha.

Her mother sighed. "I've heard stories of what they do, but I've not seen it for myself. They can heal people of many ailments. I heard about one who defeated a great beast in the shadow lands. One helped your great-great-grandfather find where to dig our well, and it has never gone dry. They travel around and teach the town leaders ways to better lead, and the town healers' ways of healing." She stopped to dry her hands and looked off in a blank stare. "There was an oracle once, whom we met on the road not far from here. I don't know if she was a gifted one, but she did place her hands on you and Taam's heads. You were an infant at that time. She said that one of you would find what she had lost and the other would tame the beast. Strange person, she was."

Sha's face lit up with a broad smile, "I was touched by an oracle?"

Her mother looked stern faced. "Sha, it was a brief moment and the lady was very odd. She didn't say anything that made sense. We don't even know what she had lost."

Sha pushed away from the table and began clearing the rest of the dishes. "So either I find something an oracle lost or I tame a wild ferocious beast."

Her mother smiled at the excitement. "Keep your visions from your friends," she paused a moment, "and your father, too. Let's keep this conversation between us." Sha nodded and continued to clean up.

Her mother went to the shelf and picked up the two figurines of her children. "Two in one house," she said quietly to herself. "I'm not sure if I'm blessed or cursed."

X

Proles

The next morning, Taam awoke to the sound of the girls sparring. He got up and leaned out the window, watching the fierce battle. One leaped in the air, kicking at the other's face. The other blocked the kick, then spun around in an attempt to knock her sister's feet out from under her as she landed. The speed of their movements was unbelievable.

Taam stepped back to the center of his chamber and mimicked some of the jabs and kicks. Then he leapt up and spun, with one leg in front of him and the other folded underneath him. He came crashing down to the floor and lay there in a heap.

How do they fight like that? he thought. It seemed they would hurt themselves as easily as they could injure their opponent.

After Taam walked around in circles long enough to stop limping, he eased out of his room and over to the stairs. Loy and Vele were not around and the twins were still locked in combat. Taam raced up the stairs so he could be on the roof when the sun rose. As he approached the library he heard voices. Taam froze, listening intently.

"Yes, King Han has made the decree," said Master Vele's voice. "It appears the clerics are shifting the winds."

"What has the council said of this?" asked Loy.

"There is a split in the council. Most want to discredit Mach publicly to gain the support of the people. A few want to obliterate the clerics all together. Those for war are few but very powerful."

There was a short silence before Loy answered. "There is wisdom in having the trust of the common man; however, I'm not sure if it will work since we've been obscure for so long. I wonder if it would breed fear instead of trust. People fear what they do not understand."

Taam began to feel uneasy eavesdropping on the conversation. He continued up the stairs, making an extra effort to step loudly so they would be warned of his presence. He stepped onto the library landing and greeted both teachers with a bow.

"I was just on my way up to greet Sol Solis," said Taam. "Would you care to join me?"

"How nice of you," said Master Vele holding her elbow out for Loy to take.

The morning was cool but not cold. Winter would be ending in a few weeks. The three stood at the wall facing east, breathing in the chill and exhaling a warm moist steam. The silence was deafening.

Master Vele broke the quiet. "What about war, Loy? How would the clerics be identified?"

"In the beginning, if they hide, one would not be able to recognize them easily," said Loy. "Some of us will be able to see through the lies, some will be obvious. Eventually their blind faith will give them away. But some common folk would be mistaken for clerics because of their faith."

The sky lightened as dawn approached. Taam began to fidget. He felt they knew he had been listening in.

"I've always felt that war was for beings of lesser comprehension," said Master Vele. "What do you think, Taam?"

Taam stood quietly for a minute, though it seemed an eternity with the others eyes on him. Dawn was almost upon them. *What must I say?* He thought. *How should I react? I'm going to look like an insolent fool.* But as the sun broke the horizon, Taam knew what to say.

He stood up straight and smiled. "I think it's going to be a beautiful day," he said. Then he rested his elbows on the wall, placed his chin in his hands, and watched the wonderful oranges and reds come to life. Night slowly evolved into day as Sol Solis took its place in the sky once again. Loy and Master Vele just smiled at each other and with a sigh; they too watched the morning come alive.

At the morning meal the teachers sat at a different table than the students. Taam sat with the twins, who discussed their sparring techniques. Their conversation eventually turned to the girls' recent journey; they had been at a school over three weeks' travel away. They had passed through six townships on the way to Arborludusium.

"Master Vele had us pass our selves off as men," said Delane.

"Men can be such swine," said Melane

"She said it was safer in the settlements this way," said Delane.

"Men should respect us for what we are," said Melane.

"Everyone should respect women," said Delane.

Master Vele taught them to be proud of who and what they were.

The school they came from was Montisludsium, which they explained meant 'school of the mountains.' Crystalline formations adorned the school and made the light do many strange things.

Melane pulled a small triangular crystal from her pocket and showed Taam. "You see this? It's called a prism. It splits the sunlight into different colors."

Taam took it and held it up to the ceiling. He turned it around, examining it.

"It only works in real sunlight," said Delane.

Taam sat the prism on the table and stared at it a moment. "Since all power comes from Sol Solis, and the light is the power, what does it do to the power of the light when it splits it?"

The two girls stared at him for a moment with blank faces, then looked at each other. "I would have never thought of that," said Melane.

"I've got a crystal in my room," said Taam. "My sister found it. Do you want to see it?"

They agreed and Taam went to get it.

When they met back in the courtyard, the two girls became very interested in the gem-like stone.

"It feels as if there is power stored in here," said Melane. She held it up to the light and peered at it with one eye closed. Delane took a turn doing the same thing.

Master Vele and Loy soon joined them and the twins showed their teacher.

"Where did you get this?" said Master Vele.

Both girls pointed at Taam and said almost in unison, "His sister found it."

"Taam, may I study this for a while?" asked Vele.

Taam nodded and she pocketed the stone.

Loy got the students' attention. "You will all be studying together for a little while. Beginning today, I will teach during the mornings and Master Vele will have the afternoons."

With that, Master Vele went up to the library and Loy took the three apprentices to the logs on the edge of the courtyard.

"Today's class will be about current events. There are things going on in the world, which will have an effect on you. And you will, in turn, affect them." Loy stood in front of the group slowly pacing to and fro. "The ruler of this land, King Han, has been taught by clerics who believe in gods. The kings who came before His Majesty were all taught by members of the Council of Elders. The Council of Elders is the governing body of what you call the gifted ones." Loy spoke as if he had given this same lecture a hundred times. "The gifted ones are the descendants of the ancient ones. We are the Proles, the descendants. There are few references to the ancient ones, but the only references which speak directly about them refer to them as Omnipotens Beatus. The words mean 'blessed by the all powerful.' The clerics see this reference as people being blessed by gods. We do not agree."

Loy stopped pacing and stood directly in front of the group with his fingers interlocked together resting on his waist. "Now, the Council has, over the years, refrained from showing commoners what people like us are capable of doing. They feel that fear about our actions would result in a revolution, which no one would win. The oracles agree with this. The clerics want the common people to know what we are capable of, and they want them to fear us. They submit that we are evil and not entirely human. In a revolution they would profit in power and even riches. In either case, the common folk lose."

Surely the clerics aren't that stupid, Taam thought. Not human? What would we be? Why would anyone want to profit from someone else's pain?

"Since King Han has been taught by the clerics, Mach, the high priest, has talked King Han into passing an edict, which requires all people to come to the cities of Mach's choosing and be counted in a census. This will allow the king to calculate his assets and impose new laws if he wishes. It will also allow the clerics to query the entire kingdom and root out who is of the Proles and who their families are."

With this the two girls gasped and looked at each other, almost terrified. They didn't say a word.

Taam knew they were thinking of their family. He, too, felt a twinge in his heart, but he didn't allow it to show. "Teacher," he said, "why wasn't King Han taught by the gifted... I mean the Proles?"

Loy looked down quickly. "The King's teacher angered His Majesty's father. King Han never even knew the Proles existed until he was a young man. The cleric teaching him found a student of the Proles and manipulated him into performing feats for the king. The student was very young, not even a man, and the outcome was devastating. The cleric teacher died. The student was executed on the spot."

Taam felt his chest tighten as the picture of an execution flashed across his mind.

XI

Heart

The three of them became restless as they gathered the composure to push on.

"What will happen to our families, Teacher?" Delane asked as a tear rolled down one of her cheeks..

"They have been notified of the danger, and are being tutored on how to reply to any question they may be asked."

"What can we do?" asked Melane.

A voice came from behind the students, clear and deep. "Finish your apprenticeship," said Master Vele. "Loy, would you join me for a short while—and bring Taam, please."

Loy, seeming puzzled at the interruption, rose and instructed the girls to practice reciting a text. He handed them a scroll. Then, with Taam in tow, he followed Vele up the stairs. The twins put their heads together, whispering.

Master Vele took the stairs two at a time. Loy had trouble keeping up with her. They entered the library and went to one of the tables. Several parchments were spread out on it. Master Vele had used bound books to hold the corners down of the smaller scrolls. Faded runes and carefully drawn figures covered almost every bit of the substrate.

Loy recognized the writings immediately. "I was just speaking of this text with the students," he said.

Vele pointed to one of the pages. "Right here—" she paused for a moment, then began to read, "...And in the dawn of the darkness there came a light. A powerful light lost unto Mundus Terra by the old sighted one. It shall be found by the young sighted one, tempered by the one strong in heart, and wielded by the one strong in mind. The light shall fill the dark and vanquish it until a living light takes its place."

"I've read this oracle account many times," said Loy.

"Yes, but you didn't know that this is the Lumen Lacertosus," said Master Vele, as she held out Sha's stone.

Loy took the stone in his hand and rubbed it between his thumb and forefinger. He carefully held it into the air. "Lumen," he said, and a shining white orb appeared above them, growing brighter and brighter. Suddenly the stone began to glow, but the light from the stone was different than that of the orb—the orb's light was dull and it seemed fabricated. The light from the stone was brighter, as if it were sunlight piercing the darkness through a hole in the wall.

If I were a cat, thought Taam, *I would want to curl up in the warmth.* The stone drew in this light, as if it fed on the orb's power until, finally, the orb had disappeared. As the light was drawn in and disappeared, the clear blue beauty of a gem once more sat perched in Loy's finger tips.

"What's going on? What just happened!" asked Taam.

"You need to go fetch your sister here," said Loy.

"And we need to find the heart referred to in the prophecy," said Master Vele.

"No," Taam firmly replied. "I will not subject my family to this or to any danger. My sister has done nothing to deserve… I mean, she has not used the powers. She is not a Proles." Taam's throat seemed to close after those words as feared he disrespected a master warrior.

Master Vele cocked her head at him. "Do you feel you're being punished for being gifted?" she asked.

Taam looked down at his boots. "No, Master, I feel overwhelmed with information and caged in this school. I like learning new things, but I've just found out that because I used a power that I didn't know existed, I've placed my family in danger. Now my sister has found some sort of weapon. I'm afraid that… I don't know."

Loy placed his hand on Taam's shoulder. "Honored Taam, son of Hym, please listen to me."

Taam looked up at Loy, embarrassed by the formal salutation.

"Most students are capable of what you can do when they are beyond twenty or twenty-five years of age. No student has honored this school by decorating it with its namesake, trees. No student has ever decorated the entire school before, just small parts. We feel you are the one the oracle's account speaks of where it says, *one of strong mind*. Your sister may be the *young sighted one*."

"Teacher, how do you know all of this?" asked Taam.

"Different people have different gifts. I am capable of communicating with the powers around us. When the trees sing, I listen. The old trees by the river told me of your oath before I met you. Your sister is watching this very conversation at this very moment. She does not understand what is happening, but she sees nonetheless. Your stone craft has passed this information to me. Your mother is also beginning to worry, because the same figures are required to let her know what is happening."

"Perhaps we should all go together," said Master Vele. "It isn't that far."

Loy agreed and Taam, knowing what Loy had said about his mother was true, also agreed. "Everyone must prepare for immediate departure," said Master Vele.

As the group began the half day journey, Master Vele told the twins what had happened.

"You mean this *boy*," said Delane, looking at Taam derisively, "whom I saw spinning across the courtyard, is spoken of by an oracle? *This* boy will save the world?"

"This man," said Taam, "who attempted a feat which has never been successful, carries a stone that *may* save the world," moving to within inches of her face and eye to eye.

Melane asked to see the stone again. Taam turned away from Delane and handed it to her sister. For a long time Melane inspected the little jewel-like stone. She held it up to the sun and looked through it, rubbed it against her sleeve, then looked through it again. She spoke to her sister about ancient words used in the text.

"The oracle wrote that the stone would be tempered by the *one strong heart* and then wielded by Taam," said Melane.

"It did not say Taam," said Delane.

"My point is, it can't be used until it's tempered. So what words of the old language would you use to harden the lumen lacertosus?" asked Melane.

"Maybe harden or to make strong," said Delane

The twins had fallen a little behind the others, so Vele stopped and called them to catch up.

The girls approached the group hand in hand, saying words in the ancient language.

"To make undefeatable," said Melane.

"We need it to be a hard stone, hard stone," said Delane.

Suddenly Loy leapt up from his resting place with both arms outstretched. His mouth was open, but no sound came out.

Taam looked at the girls, who were staring at each other intently and smiling. They were facing each other with the stone between their finger tips. They were saying something not just in unison, but as if with one voice.

Master Vele watched them, her face drained of color and her eyes opened wide.

"Silex silicis," said the girls. Taam knew it meant 'hard stone.'

He couldn't see anything else, just white light. Suddenly, he heard the girls scream out in pain. Loy made a sound as if he'd been struck in the stomach and a moan followed. He didn't hear Vele at all.

Taam closed his eyes and shielded his face from the light. He felt no pain at all but just stood there for what felt like a long time. When he finally uncovered his face, the light was still there, but now he could make out shapes on the ground. Loy and Vele were crumpled there, lying still. The twins were also lying on the ground, but their eyes were open and the both still had their hands on the stone.

The stone was a bright spot in the contours and shapes. Taam reached out and grasped it, closing his fist around it. The light instantly stopped. Surprisingly the stone wasn't hot, it felt as if nothing had changed at all.

All four of the unconscious group suddenly gasped a breath, as if they had just come out of the water.

"Stop!" yelled Loy.

"No, girls!" Master Vele wailed.

Everyone sat up and looked at each other, clearly astonished at what had just happened.

"Where is it?" asked Loy.

Taam held up his closed fist.

"It seems we have no choice in the matter," said Vele. "The heart has been chosen and the tool is tempered. The first half of the oracles account has come true. All the pieces are in place."

The group slowly rose to their feet, sore from the experience, and continued their trek again.

Loy grasped his staff and looked in the direction they were traveling. "Taam, your mother is roasting a chicken in preparation of our arrival."

Taam grew excited about seeing his family again. "Her chicken is good," he said as he slipped the stone into a pocket and hurried to the front of the little expedition. As he headed for his reunion with the family he missed so much, he couldn't get the prophecy out of his mind.

"…And in the dawn of the darkness there came a light. A powerful light lost unto Mundus Terra by the old sighted one. It shall be found by the young sighted one, tempered by the one strong in heart, and wielded by the one strong in mind. The light shall fill the dark and vanquish it until a living light takes its place."

XII

Task

Taam's family was excited to see him. He hugged Sha for an extra long time. His mother cried and his father beamed with pride. Introductions followed and the family brought out stools and benches for everyone's comfort. Sha brought bowls and the twins assisted in serving. The meal was good and the drink, supplied by Loy, was enjoyed, too.

Loy and Master Vele explained all that happened, including their knowledge of Sha's ability.

Sha's mother grasped her husband's arm. "They want to take Sha."

"She is not of the gifted ones," said Hym. The girl is not like her brother. She did not make fish leap from the river.

Master Vele explained what was happening with the king and the clerics, and the dangers which were already present.

Sha's mother grasped on to her husband's arm, "Don't let them take my Sha from me. She is all I have left."

"Taam, let me see the stone," said Sha.

Everyone stopped talking and looked at them. Taam reached into his pocket and pulled it out. Delane and Melane, who'd been standing next to Sha, moved away from her, tightly holding hands.

Taam held out his fist and Sha placed her hand beneath his, palm up. They stared at each other for a moment.

What if the bright light comes again? thought Taam. Will it harm Sha? It belongs to her—I must give it to her. He opened his fist and let the stone fall into her open hand.

Sha stood there, looking at the stone. No one had seen it since the incident on the road, not even Taam. It was jewel-like, brilliant and crystalline, with an exquisite light blue tint—much like the sky on a very hot day. Not dark blue like a winter's day. The oval shape was perfect, similar to the shape of a person's eye. Taam looked at his sister's face and thought, *The shape is identical to the shape and size of her eyes.*

Sha held it up between her thumb and forefinger high above her head. "I've found what she lost. You must tame the beast," she said to Taam. She took his hand and placed the Lumen Lacertosus in it. She leaned close to his ear and whispered, "We have the same eyes." Taam's felt himself blush, as he thought, *did she hear what I just thought.* They touched foreheads, then hugged each other again.

Taam turned to Loy, "If Sha is the young oracle then she has already performed her part of the prophecy. And if she is just an oracle, then she's not one of the Proles. I don't see a need for her to go with us if she doesn't want to."

"I think he's right, Loy," said Master Vele. It must be her choice."

"I choose to stay. I am only thirteen and with Taam traveling, my family needs me," Sha replied.

"There, she chooses to stay," said Hym. "If she chooses, when she is older, then perhaps she can go."

It was decided that the party would depart in the morning, and they spent the rest of the afternoon catching up on happenings. Taam stayed the urge to show his parents some of his abilities, but in private, he did demonstrate to Sha how to light a fire. He made her promise not to tell anyone else about it.

Taam and his father completed the cabinet for the figurines. Loy taught Taam's mother how to use a couple of local plants in some ways she didn't know. The twins spent time with Sha, talking and laughing in a warm spot behind the house. They even taught her some defensive moves. It was a productive, enjoyable afternoon and evening.

The next morning everyone was up with the sun. Taam awoke with old familiar fragrances like the quilt his grandmother had made and the odor of burned wood from the fireplace. *It feels good to be outside the school,* Taam thought.

They ate a quick meal and prepared to leave. The search to find what the oracles had meant about 'the light vanquishing the dark' had to begin. They decided to stop by Arborludusium and prepare for the journey to the Council assembly. The Council resides a long way off. The classes would continue during the trek, Loy told Taam.

When they were out of sight of the farm, Master Vele sent a message to the council by way of procella. It contained an accounting of Taam's entire schooling and all the events concerning the lumen lacertosus up to this point. She withheld Sha's identity as the young sighted one referred to in the prophecy. Both teachers felt that the Council would push for her training much harder than they had.

"Free will must endure," Loy said, "and it can be lost even with the best intentions."

By midday they arrived at the school. Loy had Taam change the décor back to the basics for the next group of students who might use the school. When everyone was packed and everything was in its place, Loy using the power of the old language copied a couple of the texts in the library and joined the group outside. As they headed to the northwest Taam wondered about the council, *I wonder if they are all as serious as Loy. I wonder if there are other students there. What if they say Sha must come? What are we going to ask them?*

XIII

Journey

The first two days of travel were through the old woods. Some of the trees were so large that, if all five of the group held hands, they could still not touch on the other side of the tree. The canopy blocked out the sun, allowing no relief from the chill. No grass grew in the gloomy darkness, just massive column-like tree trunks. Taam could hear the wind far above them, but the air was still under the canopy where they walked.

Master Vele taught the three students how to conceal themselves in such an environment. For practice one would run up ahead and move close to a tree, then the student would speak, "Dissimulo." The tree would appear to envelop their body and conceal them from sight. The others would search for them and, if they found the one in concealment, Master Vele would use the opportunity to show any mistakes they'd made and how to prevent them in the future.

Delane and Melane were not as versed in the old language as Taam. While the twins were being instructed in the old language by Loy, Master Vele instructed Taam in agility.

"You move like a plow horse, boy. Think cat!" she said.

Then he would try the exercise again, but become unbalanced, landing on his knees or various other parts of his body. He was glad the girls were busy with their studies. He was embarrassed at his inability to be as graceful as the twins.

The power within the school enabled a thought to produce substance at meal times. Out in the wood, food was not as available. Since there was no grass, the only meat was the birds and squirrels in the tall trees. Loy had taught Taam how to identify which among the sparse plant life was edible, and they gathered as they walked. Mushrooms and tubers made up the largest portion of their meals, with other plants and herbs they found at the edges of small clearings and stream banks. Clearings and streams were few in the old wood.

On the third and fourth day, they were still in the wood, but the trees were not as large and there were more clearings. With the increase in grass and small leafy plants, came an increase in larger wildlife. Taam thought some meat might be nice for a change. He rechecked his old bow in case he came upon some sign of deer. The deer eluded his hunting skill, but two rabbits did not. The five had a hot stew that evening and went to sleep satisfied.

In the middle of the night, Master Vele woke the students, shaking them one by one. She had placed her hand over their mouths as she woke each one to prevent them from speaking. Loy had put out the fire and gathered the loose equipment by the time they were awake.

"Keep quiet, pick up your packs, and follow me," whispered Master Vele. "Loy will bring up the rear." The seriousness of her voice warranted no questions, and the students reacted quickly and quietly.

Vele led the group down winding deer trails at a fast paced walk. The moon was out but was not full; the light was very dim. Occasionally, a limb would catch one of them in the face or the throat. It was about two hours before dawn when they left the camp site. It was dawn when they stopped. They gathered in a group on a low hill, overlooking the area they'd just passed through. Vele sat crouched, looking back over their path for several minutes. Loy fished out dried bread and sundried meat from his pack for everyone to eat.

Master Vele finally turned and accepted some of the food from Loy. "I don't think they're following us," she said.

The three students stared wide-eyed at her as she quickly took a couple of bites.

"We had company," she said. "I think they were attracted by our fire. They were coming toward us quietly, which was suspicious. I thought it prudent to leave."

"Do you have any idea who it might have been, Master?" asked Melane.

"No," replied Master Vele, "but in times like this, I don't want to meet the wrong people without the advantage of preparation." She took her watch post again while everyone else rested.

All through the day they moved quickly, without speaking much at all. Near mid-afternoon they changed direction to skirt a small township, taking extra care as they made their way through the surrounding farms. The group stopped under a nut tree for a few minutes and gathered from the ground.

They laughed and talked while they labored, when a voice came from above them. "Who are you?"

Taam's heart felt like it had jumped into his throat and Master Vele had her dagger out in a flash. A small round-faced boy lay across three boughs, which aligned to make a perfect platform about two times the height of a man off the ground.

All five got up and trotted away. Master Vele said to Loy, "Do it."

Loy stopped and turned. Closing his eyes, he stretched out his open palms toward the tree and said, "Memoria Extractum."

The rest of them stopped to watch. He stood for several minutes like this.

Master Vele explained, "He is removing the memory of our presence from the boy's mind. It is a difficult thing to do because Loy has to sort through the boy's recent memories to prevent a contradiction in thought. Without a balance in one's thought, one would eventually go mad."

"It's done," Loy said finally, "but we have a problem. The boy saw some clerics in town this morning and they are looking for Proles. They said they were looking for 'evil magic doers.'"

Vele and Loy both looked at the students as if to see a reaction. All three students, already aware of the dangers had no visible reaction, but Taam did feel uneasy. With that, they moved on.

The land was dryer during the next four days. There were low hills and small scattered trees. The wildlife seemed wilder here. The nighttime was full of sounds Taam wasn't used to. There were wolves howling in the late evenings and in the morning.

Master Vele seemed to be more at ease in this environment. She smiled more and walked taller than normal. Loy, on the other hand, was much more cautious. The fear of snakes seemed to haunt him. Master Vele said several times that it was too cold for them to be out, and laughed about it.

On the twentieth day the expedition arrived on the bank of a large lake. The fish were a nice break from dry tack and the foraged food Loy and Taam provided. They camped for eleven days on this shore. There was no sign of anyone in the area and they had not seen anyone for several days. Classes had been disregarded, due to the pace they traveled. Everyone was exhausted and Master Vele was sure no one followed.

Taam's studies resumed at sunrise. The Master began having her students perform repetitive exercises. All day she worked him harder than he had ever worked before. He could barely bathe himself since he was so sore from physical exertion. The next day she made him exercise his mind by incanting methods of concealment and defensive actions with his thoughts. She would not allow him to speak the language out loud, stating this would reduce his tactical advantage. The third day on the lake was the same as the first, with a physical workout using different movements. For ten days this continued, rotating physical and mental workouts. Master Vele even taught Taam to play chess without a board. He had to remember where all the pieces were and refer to their locations by coordinates.

"I thought we were supposed to be resting," Taam said to the twins one evening. "I'm more exhausted than when we arrived."

The twins were under intense training as well. Loy had them foraging for their meals as part of it. He told them that, "Mother will provide for you anywhere you are if you use the knowledge She expects you to have." During the times they weren't foraging, they were learning the old language. The scrolls Loy had copied were texts of old oracles, and the girls were in the process of memorizing and analyzing the language used in them.

On the morning of the eleventh day after arriving at the lake, they packed to leave. The group took great pains to restore the camp site to the condition it had been in before they arrived.

"We don't want anyone to know we were ever here," said Master Vele.

They skirted around the lower end of the lake, through a swamp to the other side, and into the hills beyond.

Taam overheard Loy speaking to Master Vele. "I believe you chose the path through the swamp just for me."

She laughed, "I asked the snakes to stay away from you, Loy."

Loy huffed as if he was a little irritated until he saw Taam watching, then he winked and smiled, assuring him that it was all in jest.

Two days later, they came to the edge of a white sandy hill that looked as if it drifted like snow and then patches of grass had stopped the migration. The dune rose up as tall as an average tree, and went on as far as they could see in both directions. With a running start, Vele began churning her way to the top. It took a full minute as the hill was steep and the sand allowed no traction. The twins started up next. Taam, with the assistance of the old language, gave the girls a boost, and they were at the top as fast as they could run.

Master Vele put her hands on her hips. "It's about time you used your head," she said.

Loy and Taam went up together using the same method as Delane and Melane. From the top, as far as they could see was sand.

Master Vele turned to the girls. "All right ladies, put your heads together and tell us where the power is."

The twins held hands, leaning in and touching their foreheads together. They closed their eyes and began murmuring something to each other. In a moment they stopped and pointed. "Over there," they said in unison.

Taam knew they could feel the power in objects such as the lumen lacertosus, but he had never seen the girls do this before.

XIV

Council

Standing on top of the dune, Taam reached into his pocket and pulled out the gem. Holding it up to his eye, he looked in the direction the girls pointed. There before them, not an arrow's shot away, was the entrance to a huge stone structure. It was larger than anything he had seen before. The stones were black and reached twice as high as the dune they had just traversed. The top of the wall had every other stone missing, creating the appearance of flat teeth against the sky. The heavy timber door was closed. The wood grain showed the age of each timber to equal those of the trees they had passed through during the beginning of the journey. When he moved the jewel away from his eye structure was gone.

"What is this place?" asked Taam.

Everyone looked puzzled.

"Can you see it?" asked Loy.

"Yes, with this," answered Taam, holding out the gem in his hand.

Loy took the Lumen Lacertosus and looked toward the structure. "I don't see anything," he said.

Master Vele and the twins couldn't see the castle, either. The girls said they could feel its power, though. Taam led them to the door, and when they placed their hands upon it, it allowed them to see it.

"The castle isn't usually hidden," said Master Vele.

"Inculta Pugnaculum," said Loy as he looked up at the massive structure, "the castle in the desert. I've never seen it before."

"How do we gain entry?" asked Melane.

Vele walked to the side of the door. A rope hung there, dangling from a small hole over their heads. When she pulled it, Taam heard a bell on the other side of the wall. Master Vele stepped away from the wall and waited, looking toward the top of the wall.

After five or six minutes they heard a voice from above. "Master, is that you?"

Vele stretched out her arms and yelled back, "I sent you a note. Did you conceal yourself too well to receive it?"

"You taught us well, Master. I'll open the door."

The massive doors swung open. The wood was as thick as an arm is long. As the doors were opening, the party saw a young man with both arms up, his eyes closed, chanting a simple song in the old language. Taam thought that making a song out of the words must make it easier to remember.

When the doors were open, the man bowed low in greeting. Master Vele introduced him as Tod, a student from some years back, who now served the Council. She introduced each of the group as they entered the fortress.

"Welcome to the Inculta Pugnaculum," said Tod and bowed low once again. He closed the doors with another song, and huge beams dropped down from the sides, barring the massive doors into bronze cleats. Steps rose from each side of the door to walkways on the top of the high walls.

The group turned to walk away, but Taam stood for a moment looking at the huge beams. With his mind, he easily picked one of them up a finger's width then let it gently back down. When he turned to follow, he caught Master Vele's eyes. She smiled ever so slightly and moved on as if nothing happened.

Tod took the group into a low building with a fountain in a courtyard, so they could freshen themselves. He respectfully instructed them to wait in the courtyard when they had finished washing.

As Taam splashed the water over his neck and head, he noticed a reflection of windows high above them, filled with faces. He looked up to see seven large windows surrounding the room with people softly talking and many of them with their eyes on them. Many of the people were about Taam's age and several were obviously teachers.

This must be another school, thought Taam. He noticed that the twins were attracting most of the young men's attention from above. They tossed their hair and smiled. He watched as Vele quietly scolded the girls not to bring more attention to them. They obeyed their master, but they clearly did enjoy the attention from above.

Loy gathered the students and provided a quick history of the place. "This was once a castle built by one of the king's predecessors. A drought came upon the land and many people began to starve. The king, being wise, had a second castle built in another region of the country. He did this ten years in advance of the drought, because he'd been told of the bad times to come by an old oracle. When the people could no longer sustain themselves in this region, he moved all those who wanted to go to the new castle. That is where King Han is now. A month long storm came. It caused all the sand to surround the castle. The Proles have worked for decades to push the desert back to where it is now. The Council resides here and many students visit here each year to learn from them."

Tod approached them, carrying a huge wine skin. He handed it to Master Vele. "I pay my debts, Master," he said. He turned to the group. "Please leave your packs and follow me."

They left their packs in a heap by the fountain and proceeded through the ornate doorway into a hall. Their footsteps echoed off the stone walls. It seemed endless, with doors every five or six paces. They came to a set of double doors with carvings of creatures on them—creatures Taam didn't recognize. There were horses with horns, snakes with wings and legs, and a cat with a long hair around its neck. They were painted in vivid colors and looked remarkably lifelike.

Tod pushed open the doors, stepped inside and, in a loud voice, announced the group. "Master Vele, teacher of the art of war." She stepped through the door. "Her students, Delane and Melane, the ladies of heart." The twins stepped through the door.

Taam was now able to see into the dimly lit hall. He saw the girls move to the center of the room. They curtsied, turned to the left, and walked out of sight. "Loy, son of Josiah and honored teacher of language and of medicine." Loy walked into the center of the room, bowed low, then moved over by the girls and Master Vele. Taam could see the entire room now. It had large square columns placed three to a row—nine in all. It gave the feeling of entering a hallway, but without the walls. Directly in front of him, in an elevated box, sat seven people. "Taam, son of Hym, student and wielder of the Lumen Lacertosus."

Taam barely heard the introduction. It was as if a great wind was blowing in his ears. He could feel the blood rushing through his neck and into his head. Tod stepped aside and Taam walked forward, staring at each of the Council members' faces. They all looked cold and emotionless, except one. She was an old woman with a broad smile on her face. Her eyes were bright and they looked familiar.

Where do I know her from? Taam thought. He kept his eyes on her. Stopping in the center, he bowed low. When he rose, he saw that the seven Council members had risen from their seats and each one, in turn, made a stooped bow or curtsy.

Taam went and stood by Loy. Looking up at him, Taam realized why he recognized the face of the old woman. She and Loy had the same eyes.

The Council member in the center stood up again. "We shall meet with our friends Loy and Master Vele before the evening meal. In the meantime, it is only appropriate that our new students meet with the Council in a less intimidating environment."

He clapped his hands together and everyone in the room rose and began speaking to each other. Loy stepped out of line and went up to the old woman, who had already made her way out of the box. They were soon embracing each other, and it was clear that they were indeed of the same family. Master Vele had stepped back to the entrance and immediately began conversing with Tod.

Taam and the girls stood looking at each other, not knowing what to do. The Council member who had dismissed the meeting was the first to approach them. He was a large man with clothes made of animal skins roughly sewn together. He smelled odd, like a musty cave with a little smoke mixed in. He introduced himself as Gabrel.

"I hold the position of Procer, therefore it is my honor to begin, conduct, and end the meetings. When you approach the Council while it is in session, you would speak to me. When the Council is not in session, such as now, we are simply equals."

Taam looking him in the eye. "How does one address you?"

Gabrel smiled. "You would honor me by addressing me as Procer Gabrel, or simply Procer would suffice in an informal setting." With that said the three students bowed, and the Procer turned and walked away.

The next Council man was tall and thin with white hair. The ends of his long black robes were tattered and frayed, but they were clean. He addressed the twins first, bowing to them and repeating their title of 'Ladies of the heart.' The girls blushed and curtsied back at him. He then turned to Taam saying, "Wielder of the Lumen Lacertosus." Taam returned the bow. "I am Soren. It falls to me to keep the records for the Council. If you need any writings or records, please make me aware of your needs."

"Do you have many oracle texts?" asked Delane.

"My dear, I have an entire library of them. You and your sister are welcome to read as much as you want." He smiled at them then turned to Taam, his smile lessening somewhat. "I have a book you should read, Taam. It is for your eyes and for those whom you trust. Put it away now and return it at your leisure."

He held out a small red leather-bound book, which Taam took, slipping it into a pocket and thanking him. Soren turned and walked away.

Loy approached with the old woman. "Taam, Delane, Melane, it is my honor to introduce my mother, Ora."

Ora beamed with delight and grasped each one's hands, telling them how she had been looking forward to seeing them again.

"Again?" said Melane.

"Oh my dear I met you all when you were young. I especially wanted to see Sha. She found my stone, you know. Taam, did she tell you where she found it?"

"No, I never thought to ask her," said Taam.

"No matter, we'll see her soon enough."

The two girls gasped, quickly covering their mouths. "You're the Old Oracle!"

Ora smiled broadly. "I've still got a few years left in me, ladies. Why don't you sit with me during the evening meal? I would like to see the stone once more. In the meantime, Taam, keep it in your pocket."

Loy and Ora walked away. "She certainly has a different personality to her son."

"Yes," said Melane, "she *has* one, unlike her son." They laughed as another member of the Council approached.

Joel was very old and walked slowly. His white hair was long as was his beard. When he introduced himself, he simply nodded his head, for bowing would have put him off balance. Karl on the other hand was young and inquisitive, wanting to know about their journey and adventures, yet he talked so much that the students were unable to reply. He didn't stop talking until another man joined the group, telling Karl Master Vele wished to see him. Karl smiled and reached out, touching each one's hand in turn as he excused himself to find Master Vele.

The newcomer seemed cold. He cupped a glass of wine with both hands and glared at the trio.

Taam bowed and said, "It is an honor to meet you," and the girls followed suit.

"I am Seth. When you reach the end of your training, I will be the last teacher you'll have before you are allowed to teach students of your own." He promptly turned and walked away, his long purple robes flipping up in the back as his heels caught the hems.

The last Council member approached them. She was beautiful, Taam thought—tall, slender, with long black hair flowing to her waist. She wore bands on her wrists woven from gold wires. Her robes were green like rye grass in the early fall, and they touched the floor. Her skin was very light and a gold locket adorned her chest.

"I am Andraya," she said, holding out her hand with her palm down and her fingers limp.

Taam stared at her hand wondering what to do.

Melane moved forward grasping her hand and kissing it saying, "Council Andraya, we are honored." Delane did the same, and Taam followed their lead.

"I've heard you carry the Lumen Lacertosus, Taam. Would you honor me with a viewing?"

Taam thought for a moment about pulling it out of his pocket. He looked past Andraya and saw Ora looking right at him sternly. "I would be glad to show you the beautiful gem, at the appropriate time," he said, smiling.

"Oh yes," she smiled, "please do so." She turned and walked away.

Ora smiled at him and resumed her conversation.

As Taam turned to speak to the girls, he saw Seth in a corner with his eyes fixed on them. "That's all of them I guess." Taam stared back until Seth turned disappearing behind a column.

XV

The Book

Taam sat across from Council Ora. She was very easy to talk to and asked for no special treatment. She spoke of adventures and ideas and writings of other oracles. The twins sat on either side of her, almost overwhelming her with questions. When Loy tried to settle their excitement, Ora said, "We all must learn and the best way to learn is to enjoy yourself while doing so, Loy. I am enjoying their company." Loy gave up on his attempt, happily listening, too.

The meal was a feast compared to what the group had been enduring. The company was refreshing and the small dining hall was filled to capacity. Taam was thinking, *there had to be a place where the students and other teachers were.* The table Taam was sitting at suddenly grew quiet. Taam looked up from his dish to see Ora, Loy, and the twins looking at him.

"Did I miss something?" he said.

"Would you like a tour of the castle?" Ora replied.

"Oh yes, that would be great," said Taam. They left the dining hall through a different door than they had entered.

When they came to the long hallway going back toward the fountain, a young man joined the group quietly following behind. Soon they were back at the front entrance.

Ora pointed up the stairs beside the large wooden gate. "Up there you'll get a view worth having."

The three students scampered up the stair to the top of the wall. The walkway was wide enough that all three could walk side by side. They were looking out over what was actually an entire city within the stone walls. One could walk all the way around the city while staying on the wall, though it would be a long walk. The building they had just been in was a small one closer to the front. The buildings seemed to be larger and taller in the center of the city.

It would take a week to see the entire city! thought Taam.

"There must be thousands of people living here," said Melane.

They went back down the stairway and on with the group; the tour took them next to the stables where people were taking care of fine horses and other livestock. Down a wide street, they passed shops selling everything one could want. Loy showed interest in a tinker's shop with pots and pans, and then an herbalist with plants growing all over the front of the store. The twins pressed their faces to a clothier's, then a dressmaker's shop. The armory seemed to interest the young boy who was still tagging along with the group. There was a small square in front of the largest building in town. Farmers had their winter harvest and swine, among other livestock, for sale. It reminded Taam of the time he and his father had taken their various crops to town.

The building at the far end of the square was massive. It was adorned with giant carved figures similar to those on the council chamber doors. The corners of the building had round towers higher than its walls.

"That is where the king used to live," said Ora. "When a prince was born, a Proles would be summoned to begin teaching him in his first few days of life. You know his first few years of training shaped his entire outlook on life."

Delane stepped forward, looking at the building closely. "Does anyone live there now?"

"Oh no, that would be disrespectful to King Han. It is his house, you see."

"Can he tell one to leave the city?" asked Melane.

"Yes, he could, if he knew the place existed."

"How can he own it if he doesn't know it exists?"

"Well Melane, it has been several generations since a king lived here. We were given the honor of taking care of the place until the king saw fit to take possession of it again. It has never been spoken of again. However, there are records in the king's library which could start him looking for it. We know it is his; we respect it as such. We don't offer the information to everyone, especially Mach."

The young tag-a-long went up to Ora and whispered in her ear.

"Oh my," she said. "This is my page, Sean. He has reminded me that you must obtain quarters. Let us go back to the hall." Sean was a good-looking young man of fourteen or fifteen. He wore a red sleeveless smock like a uniform over his clothes. A matching red sash tied around the smock, making it form to his body.

Upon nearing the hall Sean ran ahead, and by the time the group entered the long hallway Tod was coming toward them with Sean on his heels. "Your quarters are this way," he said, turning in through a doorway and entering another hallway. The doors in this hallway had small wooden plaques with names carved into them. Each person had their own cubiculum, just as it was in Arborludusium.

Ora took Loy by the arm. "You need to stay here with the boy," she said quietly. Loy nodded.

Tod and Ora excused themselves, and Sean bowed and followed behind his master.

Taam began to open his door, but Loy pulled him aside. "You stay in my room tonight," he whispered. "I sense something is not right." Taam nodded and went into Loy's room, latching the door behind him.

He pulled the gem from his pocket and scanned the room, but did not see anything unusual. There was a bed, a table with two chairs, a wash basin, and chamber pot. He pulled out the small book Soren had given him, sat at the table, and opened it. The pages were blank.

Why would Soren give me a blank book?

Thinking that the text might be hidden by the power, Taam tried some of the old language. "Protractus," he said quietly, yet nothing happened.

"Aperio."

"Patesco."

"Ostendo."

Nothing was happening. Taam thumbed through all the pages, closed the book, and put it on the table. He stared at it. Caressing the rough leather cover, he noticed an indention in the spine. Inspecting it closely, he noticed that the Lumen Lacertosus would just fit in the place. He took the gem from his pocket and set it in the space. It fit perfectly and was held snugly in place.

Taam opened the book, once again displaying the title page. It was written in the old language— *Lumen Lacertosus Omnipotens Beatus.*

"Powerful Light Blessed by the All Powerful," Taam said to himself. "This as a book about the stone. This is just what I need. It's also going to be dangerous having them together though. If the stone is as powerful as everyone thinks, a book about it would give someone the knowledge of how to use that power."

The first chapter covered the origin of the Lumen Lacertosus. It had entered the world as a tear of Sol Solis, striking the ground with a fire and force never seen before. It had lain in that place for many years. A lake formed at the spot it had struck, and the water was clear to the bottom. A girl swimming in the lake had been drawn to its power and, diving deep, scooped the stone from the bottom. In time the girl became a woman and the power of the stone empowered her to accomplish great things and gave her long life. The woman's name was Ora.

The second chapter covered the powers of the stone. Ora had been empowered as an oracle seeing the future. She was able to manipulate the power of Mundus Terra without knowing the old language. Through the stone, anything manipulated was revealed to her. *"That explains why I could see the castle through the gem."* thought Taam. *Ora is the old oracle and she must have lost the stone. Maybe the stone is why I can manipulate the power without saying the words.*

In the third chapter, he read that, after the stone became tempered, its powers would increase. Tempering would occur when a bond of love was passed through the stone. It would repair the fractures caused when it struck Mundus Terra. This would allow it to focus power through it and become a source of incredible power.

A knock came from the door, startling Taam. He closed the book, pulled the gem from the niche in the cover, and put them in separate pockets.

Taam opened the door and let Loy into the room. They sat down at the table.

"Have you seen anything unusual since we've been here?" said Loy.

Taam thought about it for a moment. "Not anything more unusual than everything over the past few months."

Loy smiled. "I guess that is as honest a reply as possible."

"Teacher, your mother is on the Council, and is the Old Oracle. Why do you keep me in the dark?"

Loy looked down at the table. "I'm sorry, Taam. I do it to protect you. I've been a teacher for many years and I don't want you to be confused by knowledge which should not apply."

"What do you mean, Teacher?"

Loy sighed. "Taam you must learn many things on your own so as not to be swayed by my opinion or anyone else's opinion."

Taam sat thinking about this statement for a moment as Loy continued.

"There are some things I do need to fill you in on. My mother trusts Sean, as she does Procer Gabrel and Council Soren. I trust Master Vele, and she trusts Tod. The people we distrust, we will keep to ourselves, so you may make up your own mind."

"Council Soren has given me a book."

"Yes, I know—my mother wrote the book. When you finish reading it, you need to get it as far from the stone as possible, or destroy it. Together they are a treasure valuable beyond imagination."

Loy gave Taam his pack, which Tod had delivered from the fountain. "Stay obscured from sight," said Loy. He exited the room and Taam latched the door.

After preparing for bed, Taam placed the book inside his clothes. With the old language, he suspended himself near the ceiling and obscured his body from the vision of anyone who might enter the room, then drifted off to sleep.

XVI

Young Oracle

Sha sat high in a tree on a thick bough, watching the road from town. She didn't know exactly what to look for, so she was watching for any and everything. Something was going to happen—she could feel it deep inside. Through her dreams, she had been watching the training Taam and the twins had been receiving on the bank of a lake. She had been matching the repetitive exercises Master Vele had given her brother, blow for blow and step for step. Her abilities had begun to flourish, maybe even faster than her brother's.

This morning she had been kicking an acorn from one foot to the other for about a half an hour, when she saw a movement and froze. The acorn fell to the ground. On the road in the distance a group of people walked in two columns. They wore smocks of the same dingy yellow trimmed in red, and they carried long poles.

Sha leaned forward, slid off her perch, and dropped to the next limb. She caught it with her hands and swung around and up to another horizontal limb several cubits away. Then she dropped the short distance left, landing flatfooted on the ground below, flexing her knees to gracefully cushion her landing. "I wonder why Taam doesn't get that, it's so easy." Off to the farm she ran.

Sha entered the tiny farm house and saw her mother stuffing essentials into bags. Her mother looked up at her. "How long?"

"Not long, perhaps half the thickness of a finger," was Sha's reply. Without a method of telling time, the movement of the sun across the sky at an arm's length made a finger's width about half an hour at this time of the year.

"Take this bag and get your father from the east field."

Sha did as she was instructed. In a very short time the family was skirting around the edge of the farm, quickly walking with the bags and packs. They had been prepared for this since Taam's last visit.

"Mother, how did you know I was coming?" asked Sha.

Her mother reached in her pocket and pulled out the figurine of Sha. "I know what all of you are doing all the time, my love."

Sha smiled with pride, thinking what a special family she had.

Hym led the group and Sha followed at the rear. Both her parents glanced back frequently to make sure she wasn't falling behind. Most of the time, they traveled on deer trails, staying off the road. Loy had told them where to go and that it would take a day and a half to get there. He'd given Hym landmarks to follow, since he had not traveled in this area before. They stopped as few times as possible to rest, and they traveled until it was too dark to travel anymore. That evening they made camp under a giant holly tree. They ate rations that Sha's mother had made for the trip and slept.

When the farmer and his wife woke they found Sha standing at the edge of the clearing with a Holly branch in each hand staring up into the sky. They went to her side and followed the direction of her gaze. "What are you looking at?" asked Hym.

There was no response.

"Look at her eyes," said her mother.

Sha's eyes were wide open and glassy. Her mouth hung open with a slackness in her jaw—as if she were completely relaxed. Her parents looked closely at her but refrained from touching her. She breathed slowly with a very little foggy mist coming from her mouth in the cool morning.

The farmer and his wife stood staring at their child, not knowing what to do for several moments. Finally, Sha closed her mouth and looked down at her mother, who was now kneeling in front of her, tears streaming down her face.

"Mother, why are you crying?" asked Sha.

Her mother didn't reply. She just reached up and embraced her child as if she had just returned from a long voyage. Her father, who sighed heavily with a great deal of relief, hugged them both briefly then rose and began packing up the camp site.

"Mother, I've been listening to a song the holly tree has been singing. It's told me some things we need to know."

"We have to go," said Hym. "Let's get packed and move along." Sha's mother left her standing and began breaking up a small loaf of bread.

Sha walked up to her father, who was now tying up a bed roll, and placed her hand on his shoulder. "Father, the holly told me that the group of soldiers passed our home without stopping. And that I should teach you some of the things I have recently learned."

Hym's eyes revealed some of his fear. "I don't know what to believe anymore. I've seen things I thought were not possible. I've been told of dangers that exist, which I have reason to believe are real. I don't know what to think."

Sha's mother moved to her husband's side. Standing behind him, she took hold of his shoulders. "This is a time you should trust in your daughter, my love. Let us listen to what she has to say."

Hym stood and they both moved to a large protruding root to sit side by side. "Go ahead Sha," he said. "What is it the tree wants us to know?"

Sha took one of the branches she was still holding and carefully removed all the twigs and leaves from it until it was one slightly crooked stick. "Taam has the gift to manipulate the powers of the world, as he and Loy explained to us. None of us have the gift to do this. The holly has informed me that we do not need the gift to manipulate the power. We can do it by focusing the energy around us through something else with the gift—such as a wand made from a tree which was alive when the stone Taam carries arrived. Taam taught me to push the energy through myself and out of my hands to create fire. He said to picture it happening in my mind and say the word ignis. I couldn't do it no matter how many times I tried. But now…" She turned and pointed the stick at a small clump of dry grass and said, "Ignis".

The clump of grass crackled, smoldered, and became engulfed in flame.

Her mother gasped. "How did you, I mean where did, uh, put it out!"

Sha stepped on the small fire, extinguishing it, and handed the wand to her mother. "You try it."

Her mother took the wand, pointing it carefully at another clump. "Ignis?" she said. Nothing happened.

"Mother, do you believe you can do it?" asked Sha.

Her mother lifted her face with a look of offense, pointed the wand again, and said the word rapidly, as if anger motivated the statement. A small thin line of fire shot from the wand, engulfing the clump and incinerating it in an instant. She flipped the wand around and held it in front of Hym with an expression of satisfaction on her face.

Hym took the wand in his hand and looked at it for a long time. Finally he looked up at his young daughter. "I'm not so sure there is wisdom in common folk learning the secrets of the gifted ones. There is a great deal of training received by the gifted ones before they are taught to wield such power. The power is a gift and we shouldn't abuse the gifts. They don't belong to us."

Sha responded immediately. "Father, we are in danger. I've watched the training of Taam, Delane, and Melane for a long time. I can do things like make myself disappear if danger comes—can't we use this in our journey?" She continued more sarcastically, "Would it be abuse if we were hurt or killed?"

"Sha!" said her mother. "Respect your father!"

Hym handed Sha the wand. "Let's finish packing and we'll speak of this another time."

Sha packed her bedroll and tucked the wand into her tunic. As they left, Sha's mother picked up the other holly branch. Keeping her actions concealed, she removed the twigs and made another wand and hid it in her clothing.

The trio traveled on as before, staying on the wildlife trails. Sha was in the center of the column, walking with determination in her step. She had to get her father to understand, but she wasn't sure how.

By midmorning they had reached the edge of a stream. Both Sha and her mother sat on a flat rock on the edge of the stream, letting their feet dangle in the cold water. Hym walked upstream to find a way to cross, as the river here appeared very deep.

While her husband was gone, Sha's mother quizzed her about the different words she'd learned and what they meant.

Sha explained, "*dissimulo* is used to conceal. It will allow the person to be engulfed by the object they stood next to. Taam and the girls would stand by a tree and let the trunk hide them from view. My favorite is *peragro*, which allows one to walk through solid objects. I can't be locked away if I have my wand, I could just walk through the wall."

Sha had observed several of the defensive words taught by Master Vele and described them in detail to her mother.

"The soldiers were not coming for us," continued Sha. "They passed the farm without stopping."

"You must teach me what you know, but respect your father by not bothering him with this. Your father, as do so many others, fear what he doesn't understand. I, as your mother must protect you at all costs."

When Hym returned, they proceeded upstream to a fallen tree where crossing was safe. On the path, while no one was aware, Sha's mother performed the act of concealment using her own wand. She watched as Sha turned to look, but knew her daughter couldn't see her. As Sha moved on a few more steps, she brought herself back into view, so when her daughter turned again and saw her she thought nothing of the incident. In her mind she went over all the words her daughter had taught her so as to commit them to memory.

That afternoon brought the family to a cottage with an acorn carved on the transom. "This is the place Loy described," said Hym.

They stopped at the gate and announced themselves. Soon, an old man came out of the house and peered at the tired group. "Come in, you are welcome here. Loy told me you would be coming." The old man turned and walked back in, leaving the door standing open. Hym and his family hurried in behind him.

The cottage was small, as they all were. The room was cluttered with furniture of the type made by craftsmen. Sha had never seen such finery, since everything they owned, they'd made with their own hands. The little tabletops were smooth and oiled to a shine. The wall along one side was lined with shelves containing parchment scrolls and square stones with runes on them. It was obvious that the man was learned.

The man walked to the stove and retrieved a small kettle. "We shall introduce ourselves and then we shall sit and have some tea. I am Josiah," he said and bowed.

Hym introduced himself, returning the bow. Then he introduced his family and thanked Josiah for his hospitality. He presented a gift of sourdough bread.

"Loy asked me to help you. In truth, I think you will help me more than I will help you," said Josiah. But first, let us have tea and rest your traveling legs."

They sat for tea and Hym explained about the soldiers and the trek to his cottage. He left out the part concerning the holly tree.

Josiah listened intently, but hardly spoke. He picked up the empty tea set and took it to the kitchen. With that, he directed the girls to the kitchen and Hym to the back garden where they worked till just before dusk. The little house couldn't have held another soul, but they were all glad to sleep somewhere that night for exhaustion had set in.

XVII

Josiah

The group rose in the morning just after the sun. Josiah was already up, sitting in the back garden on a stone bench drinking a cup of bitter tea sweetened with honey. As Hym and his wife came out to the garden, Josiah offered them a cup.

Josiah directed them to places to sit. "I think we can sit and speak for a while since my work is caught up. I thank both of you for your hard work yesterday."

The two acknowledged the thanks gracefully.

Josiah continued, "I noticed that your daughter carries a twig from the great holly tree. Do you know why?"

There was a long silence before Hym answered. "The tree spoke to her. It gave her a means to protect herself from dangers which may arise."

"I see," said Josiah. "You have been thinking about this for a while." He took another sip of his tea. "How do you feel about this, Hym?"

Hym took his time thinking about the question, taking a long drink from his tea. "Well sir, I'm not sure. I wonder if it is wise to have such abilities with neither training nor maturity."

All three sat for a long time without speaking. Then Josiah asked, "Did Loy tell you why our king was not taught by one of the Proles?"

"No," they answered together.

Josiah told them the story of the student and the king and how the student killed the cleric teacher by misspeaking a word. "That student was Jeci, my son and Loy's brother. Jeci's death was directly caused by a lack of knowledge. That is why Loy takes his teaching so seriously. Your son could have no better teacher. I would strongly suggest that you let your daughter be taught by the Proles."

Hym and his wife looked at each other, then she asked, "Can you teach us?"

Josiah looked at her puzzled. "Us?"

She looked down at the ground and slowly pulled her wand out of her frock. "Yes, us."

Josiah emptied his cup with a small gulp, then refilled it from the small copper tea pot. "I am not one of the few gifted ones. My sons were because of my wife. The gift is passed down through the lineage, you know. You should approach the Council with your request for the knowledge."

"Why are our children gifted when we show no gift ourselves?" asked Hym.

"I don't know the answer to that question. I know that your daughter has different gifts than your son. The training she'd receive would be different to Taam's. I will send a message to the Council and ask them for guidance," said Josiah.

"When I saw my son's gift, I told the apothecary. I knew he was taught by the gifted ones and he arranged the meeting with Loy. How will you send this message?" asked Hym.

"Ah, I remember that. The apothecary came to me, too. Come, I will show you." The three walked around the house to the front door.

"Do you see the seed of the oak above the door on the transom?" said Josiah. "It is made from the same tree as the staff Loy carries. Loy has the ability to listen to the growing things around him, much like Sha. I will make my request here to the seed, and Loy will hear it wherever he is. It works much like a wand, except it is limited to communicating with Loy. I have no access to any power you see."

He began, "Mighty Quercus please whisper to my son these words. Sha and her mother, through the council of the great Holly Tree, have been granted access to powers through gifts of wands. They wish to learn to manipulate the power as does the Omnipotens Beatus Proles. What council does your Mother give?" Josiah turned to them and said. "Done. Let us breakfast and enjoy the day—it will be some time before we receive a reply."

They entered the house to find Sha curled in the corner, knees to her chin and her arms wrapped around her legs. She was sobbing and rocking back and forth. Her mother lurched forward to consol her, but Josiah stopped her before she could get to her daughter.

"Child!" he said sternly. "What have you done?"

Sha looked up at him and pointed shakily to an old, square stone tablet on one of the shelves.

Josiah reached up, took the tablet off the shelf, and ran his fingers over the runes carved into it. "Of all the writings I have, it's interesting that you would choose this particular one, Sha. What attracted you to it?"

Sha had stopped sobbing now and just sniffled as she shrugged her shoulders.

"Do you know what this tablet says?" continued Josiah.

She shook her head.

"This is a tale of a great beast and a hunter. Come sit with me in the garden and I shall read it to you. But if you can't read it, why did it scare you, child?"

"When I touched it, it- it screamed," stammered Sha.

Josiah smiled. "Yes, my dear child, it would. You are an oracle—you hear things we don't. It may have been the feeling of the scribe you heard, or perhaps a character being injured. You'll know when it is time. Don't fret, dear Sha. This is what the writings say:

"Long ago there was a hunter. He hunted in the hills among the scrubby trees using his bow, arrows, and blade of stone. He hunted mostly small animals to eat and used their fur to stay warm. He called the land his own and considered it a gift, for the land gave him what he needed to live. He never took more than he needed.

"In his land there lived huge beasts that roamed the territory. They were vicious and strong. They could eat almost anything, and the thorny brush and sharp rocks did not pierce their skin, for it was tough. These beasts had good senses, and the hunter couldn't seem to get close enough to kill one. They had the ability to move quietly and would sneak up on the hunter in an attempt to kill him. The beasts were territorial and they felt the hunter was trespassing in their space.

"The hunter tried to snare the great beasts, but they were so large his snares could not hold them. They destroyed the snares and the scrubby trees they were attached to. The hunter spent three days digging a pit to capture one. He then covered it with small branches and grass and made it appear as natural ground, but the beasts were too aware and wily. They did not fall into the trap.

"One day the hunter was stalking a bird for his supper. It was a fat one with dark feathers and was very hard to follow, since its feathers were a similar color to the surrounding brush. The hunter was so focused on the bird, he was not aware of the great beast which had begun stalking him. The beast had tusks as long as a hand. They curled upward and were sharp as flint. The beast was just beginning his charge when the hunter heard him and leapt out of the way. The beast swung his mighty head up—just high enough to cut the hunter's calf. The hunter quickly ran, darting through the brush and up some jagged rocks to safety.

"The beast stood at the bottom of the stone hill, snorting and bellowing in his success at outsmarting the hunter. He soon left and went about his normal activities, leaving the injured hunter to his pain. The hunter was angry but he also respected the beast and his abilities. No other animal was as adapted to the land as this one, and no other animal had frightened him as this one did. Not even the large predator cats had come as close as this beast.

"When the hunter had healed, and the days become longer than the nights, he set out on a journey. An old woman had told him of a mystical person who lived in the hills by a spring. This person was called Honestus because of her beauty. The name means 'beautiful and proper.' It was said that Honestus was wise and had the power to make things change.

"The spring was located many days walk to the north, where the trees became taller than four men in height. There were many dangers on the way and two wide rivers to cross. The hunter picked up hard stones for arrow heads at the first river and some stones that sparkled as a gift for Honestus. He found a root that would clean the grass stains from his hands and took it as a gift also. All along the journey he chose gifts for Honestus from the lands he passed through. He planned to ask her for a gift in return. He wanted an advantage on the beast in his land.

"Upon crossing the second river, he saw the trees were as large as they were beautiful. He was awed by the abundance of water as it came out of the rolling hills and flowed into lush meadows. The deer grazed everywhere as if they had no fear. Fruit grew on some of the trees. This was very different for a hunter used to digging roots. The sun dried up any fruit on the trees where he lived.

"Finally he arrived at the home of Honestus. It was a beautiful place where the icy cold water bubbled up knee-high in a clear pool and flowed down a stony gap into a flowery meadow below. The sound of the water was loud, but it relaxed the nervous hunter a little. He knew this was the place—it was just as the old woman had described.

"He called out to Honestus, for she was not in sight. She did not answer, so he decided to prepare for her return. He set up his camp out of the way and placed all his gifts on a flat rock. He then washed and ate some dried meat, then settled back and fell asleep.

"The hunter awoke as Honestus approached and he rose to meet her. He gestured to her in respect and smiled to let her know he was there on a friendly task. She was truly a beautiful person, yet she did not smile back, as she knew things were not always as they appeared. She was respectful back to the hunter, as that is the way it should be.

"The hunter and Honestus sat down and ate bread together and drank sweet water. When the meal was eaten, he told her the story of the great beast and the scar on his calf. He told her how the beast ruled the land, and how he needed an advantage to keep from getting hurt again. He presented the token gifts to her supplied to him by the land on his perilous journey to see her. He knew of her power to make things change and flattered her.

"After she listened, she smiled and said he should not speak of this anymore that evening. They sat back and admired the stars, spoke of tales and fables, then retired to their own camps to sleep.

"When the hunter awoke the next morning, Honestus was not there. He waited all day till she returned just before dusk. They broke bread and drank sweet water. She began to speak, 'The land has been honored by you, as you are always thankful for what you receive. And the beast was honored by you, as you respect the beast for what he is. What you are asking for, you already have. You have come to me with trinkets and flattery in an attempt to tame me. I am not the beast you need to tame.'"

Josiah put the tablet on his lap and looked at Sha. "Now do you know who screamed?"

"Yes," Sha replied. "It was Taam who screamed."

XVIII

Gryphon

Taam awoke slowly. His mouth was dry and his eyes were crusted. Hanging suspended in the ceiling of his cubiculum all night had not been as comfortable as he thought it might be. Releasing the power, he allowed himself to be lowered to the floor. From the months in the Arborludusium he knew it was a little while before dawn. He quickly prepared to leave his quarters, placed the book in his blouse, and spoke words of concealment to prevent anyone from finding it on him.

Taam opened his door as quietly as he could and peered down the hallway. No one was around. He went down the hall to the main corridor and was soon outside. The darkness was illuminated only by the stars. It was long past the setting of the moon. Making his way up the stairs by the gates, he noticed a familiar smell. He topped the flight and leaning against the wall facing east was Loy, holding two cups of tea.

"You're not late. I like that about you," said Loy.

"You brought tea, I like that about you, Teacher," replied Taam.

Loy smiled and passed a cup to Taam. He stood and watched the sky change from the dark blue shadow world through the full range of oranges and reds until the sun peeked over the

111

horizon. The border between the desert sand and the low trees seemed to create a magical barrier with conflicting textures and outlines which slowly came to life.

In the trees small columns of smoke were rising high into the sky, then slicing away from the desert as if a wind high above dragged them away. Taam strained his eyes to see where the smoke was coming from. A half league away, an encampment of soldiers sprawled across a hill. They must have made camp in the night. Loy and Taam could see no activity.

Taam pulled the gem from his pocket and looked through it at the camp. At first nothing looked odd. Then something moved at one end of the camp. It was a creature which they could not see with the naked eye.

"Teacher, they have an animal with them. I've never seen anything like it!"

"Describe it to me," said Loy.

"It is a large bird with… the body of a large cat. It's big—" He turned and looked at Loy. "It has wings and its feet are like a giant bird's!"

Loy looked out towards the camp. "They're looking for the castle and they've brought a Gryphon." Changing his tone from relaxed to alarmed, "Taam, go to the chambers. Wake Tod and anyone else you can find. Tell them the king's men are here. Then wake the twins and meet me in the stables."

Taam hurried to the council chambers. There, on the door above the group of carved creatures was a likeness of the very creature he'd just seen.

Could all these creatures be real? What is it capable of doing? he thought. He couldn't see it without the Lumen Lacertosus. Could it see the castle? He pushed the doors open and looked around the empty chamber.

"Tod!" he yelled. He moved to the center of the room and yelled again.

A door in the corner of the room to the left of the Council's seats opened and Tod appeared. "What is it, sir?"

"The king's army is here, and they have a gryphon!" replied Taam.

"Are you serious?"

"*Yes!*" said Taam. "Loy said you must warn the Council immediately."

Taam ran back down the hall to the quarters and knocked on the twin's doors. They seemed to wake much more slowly than Taam thought they should. He was soon hammering their doors with the bottom of his fist and yelling their names.

When they answered, they were already dressed. "What did you do, dress before you answered the door?" asked Taam.

"You can never be too careful," said Delane in a manner that sounded much like Master Vele's.

"We must meet Loy in the stable. The king's army is here," said Taam. He whirled and began sprinting up the corridor. The girls were right behind him. When they entered the main hallway, it was obvious that Tod was good at his job. The hallway was heavy with traffic.

They entered the courtyard and turned left toward the stables. As they approached, they saw Loy standing in the main door and Maser Vele approaching with a group of warriors. Taam was thinking he should have finished reading that book. With the power of the stone he might have known more about how to wield it. When they entered the stables there was a bustle of activity.

"You three find a place in the back of the stables. Find an empty stall," said Loy.

After explaining to the girls what Loy and he had seen, Taam settled in for a long wait. They were well out of sight, so Taam pulled the gem and the book out and fixed the jewel in place on the book's spine. He sat on the floor with the twins on either side reading along with him.

The fourth chapter explained how the stone could be used to extend the power of manipulation. Anything visible through the stone could be exposed by focusing the energy through the stone. Any manipulation focused through the stone was limited by the line of sight. This meant one must be able to see what one focused on.

The fifth chapter spoke of how the stone affected living things with which it came into contact. People who touched the stone received benefits from it. The benefits would be different for each person. Also, any living thing which was alive when the stone arrived was affected.

With this information, Melane gasped. "The gryphon would have been alive when the stone arrived. I've read it in a text somewhere. A gryphon can be thousands of years old. It will have the powers of the stone. It may be able to see the castle."

Taam closed the book and pulled the gem from its cover. Pocketing both, he went to the stall gate and looked for Loy. He was near the main door, speaking with his mother.

"Teacher!" he yelled.

When Loy saw him he motioned him over.

Taam quickly bowed to Ora. "Teacher, the gryphon will have the power of the stone. He will be able to see the castle."

"Ah, I see you've been reading the book my mother wrote," was Loy's reply.

Taam looked at Ora, embarrassed. He looked down at his feet. "Not only does it receive its power from the stone, but it is thought that the stone may be able to remove the gryphon's powers—or even kill it—"

"It is a she," interrupted Ora. "The males have no wings, son."

Both Loy and Taam looked at her wide-eyed.

"Taam, take the Lumen Lacertosus to the wall," said Loy. "Look through it and find the gryphon. Focus the energy through the stone and onto the beast. Remove its concealment. When the army sees the gryphon, they may turn on it and the clerics who control it."

Taam looked at the top of the wall, which was thick with people looking for the gryphon. "Can we clear the wall? I need to keep control of the stone and I've never used it in this manner before."

From behind Taam, Master Vele spoke up. "Tod! Clear the wall!"

In a flash, the man was up the stairs and directing everyone down. A group of warriors moved to the bottom of the stairs. They began directing people away and preventing others from going up. When the wall was almost empty, Taam started for the stairs.

"Taam," warned Loy, "don't allow the castle to become visible, if you can."

Taam nodded and headed up to the top of the wall.

The columns of smoke were no longer rising as before. The camp was beginning to pack up its tents, and the soldiers were preparing to move. Taam looked at the far left side of the camp where he had last seen the gryphon. The clerics who had been near it earlier were not there now. He scanned the camp's edge for the group of men with purple robes. He looked up and down the border of the sand. There they were, walking in a straight line into the desert, a third of a league ahead of the soldiers. Taam reached into his pocket and grasped the stone.

Loy and his mother were still standing in the stable door, watching. Vele was halfway up the stairs crouched and ready to spring to Taam's aid.

Loy looked at his mother. "Father is asking for your council, Mother. It seems the old holly tree has given Sha and her mother branches and taught them to use the power through them. They now want to learn—"

Suddenly, from above they heard Taam scream in excruciating pain. As everyone looked up, Taam flew over them, facing up. Blood streamed from his shoulders. One hand was in his pocket and the other flailed limply out to the side. He sailed over the city and disappeared into the desert.

XIX

Tame the Beast

As Taam's fingers wrapped around the gem, he heard a blast of air. Huge talons pierced his shoulders as the gryphon grasped him with her front feet, pulling the shocked youth into the air. But the moment the gryphon touched Taam, she became visible to him. It was just like when the group had touched the walls of the castle—it became visible to those who touched it.

The wind rushed past Taam and every time the beast's wings came down, he and the beast surged forward. The pain was almost unbearable and his mind was in a fog. He remembered when he almost froze his feet in the stream and thought. *I'll try to deaden the pain.*

With the old language, he thought of what to say and focused on the pain. The gryphon screamed a horrible sound, as if she was feeling the same pain as Taam. He could feel himself freefalling and the gryphon was rapidly getting farther away from him. Looking down and thinking in the old language, he slowed his descent making a soft landing in the sand below. The pain was gone and the bleeding had stopped but the weakness and inability to move consumed him. Taam collapsed in the sand.

When he opened his eyes, the sun was high and it was getting hot. He slid a hand up to his shoulder and felt the dry blood on his blouse. Both of his shoulders were stiff and throbbed with a dull, deep pain. With great effort, he sat up. Looking around, he saw the gryphon off to his right.

She was sitting on her hindquarters, licking her front feet. She was huge, with the head of a falcon and a beak large enough to snap off a man's arm. Her feathered neck was sleek, and the transition from feathers to fur was smooth at the bottom of her heaving chest. The beast's back was that of a powerful lion, all the way down to the tail, which gently flicked back and forth. She didn't acknowledge the stunned young man in any way.

Carefully, Taam checked his pockets to make sure he hadn't lost the gem or the book. They were both there. He reached into his pocket and grasped the jewel in his hand. He closed his eyes and shook his head. He heard buzzing and it was getting louder—it was as if someone was yelling at him through a long tube now.

"Who is it?" he said aloud.

"Taam, tame... it can't... hear me. Taam," said the voice.

"What did you say? I couldn't make it out," he answered.

He looked at the gryphon, but it wasn't her.

The voice was barely audible. "Taam, tame the beast, it can't be killed, do you hear me?" came the voice again.

"Sha? Is that you?" asked Taam.

"Tame the beast, Taam," said the voice.

"Sha, where are you?" asked Taam.

"I'm with Loy's father. Now, use the stone and tame the beast."

He looked at the gryphon then down at his open hand. The Lumen Lacertosus sat in his palm surrounded by dried caked blood.

I guess I need to talk to her, thought Taam. I wonder if she can understand me.

"I hear your thoughts, noble boy," said a clear voice as if it shared his body. The deep female voice was inside his mind and the words were in the old language. "You forced me to carry your pain, boy."

"Why did you attack me?" asked Taam.

"Because, you saw me," came her reply.

"You attacked me because I saw you? What kind of a reason is that?" asked Taam disgusted.

"You had not touched me, boy, yet you could see me. It is the only defense that works against men."

"How did you know I saw you?"

"Are you dense boy? I hear your thoughts. You were going to try to harm me with the Lumen Lacertosus. You were going to expose me." They sat staring at each other for a long time.

"I see that you travel with the clerics and do their bidding," said Taam.

"I am forced to," she said. She stood on all four feet and allowed Taam to see the gold bands clasped around her rear ankles. "When the master calls me back, I must go or suffer great pain. I am to lead them to the lost city."

Taam stared at the bands. I wonder if I could use the gem to remove them? he thought.

The gryphon cocked her head a little to one side. "Are you speaking to me, boy?"

"Oh, my apologies… I forgot you hear my thoughts," answered Taam. "Do you think it would be possible for me to release you?"

The gryphon stretched out her neck, looking hard at Taam. The voice in his head taunted him. "Are you sure you remember how to use it? You do seem to have a short memory."

Taam stood up. "If I released you, what would you do?"

"If you are capable, boy, and if you were to accommodate me, I would leave this land to its own demise and return to my own," replied the gryphon.

"When I release you, I wish to speak to you again before you leave. Will you do that?"

"Yes," said the beast, standing on her hind legs. She rose up in front of Taam.

He focused all the thoughts in his mind on the Lumen Lacertosus and the task at hand. After several tries the gryphon began working with him, helping him come up with untried words and phrases. Taam held the stone up to the sun, allowing it to absorb tremendous power. When he spoke the right phrase, the stone absorbed all the light around them and it was as if it were night for a moment. Then the white light flashed from the stone, striking the two bands. They fell into the sand.

In that very instant, the huge beast was off the ground and pounding the sky with her wings. "I'll see you soon, boy. You have much to learn. Do not return to the lost city until night."

"Why? Where are you going?" called Taam.

There was no answer.

Judging by the sun's position, it appeared as if it were midday, and Taam was beginning to develop a thirst. The castle was nowhere to be seen and there was no shade. He decided to take her advice and wait; it would be cooler at night anyway. Pulling the book out and setting the gem in its place, he took a second look around for soldiers, and then settled down to read.

As he completed the fifth chapter, he noted a warning:

Do not use the stone to create objects of power. Creatures that are created naturally have their own gifts. Objects created unnaturally will have an opposite effect and, instead of manipulating power, they will cause power to cease existence.

I wonder if that's what the gryphon was talking about when she said she would leave this land to its own demise. thought Taam.

"Taam, you tamed the beast, I knew you could!" said Sha's voice in his head.

"Sha? Is that you?" asked Taam out loud.

"I saw the whole thing," replied Sha, "and I'm glad we can talk. I need to go now, but I'll contact you later."

"Sha? Sha... Sha, *answer me*!" yelled Taam.

There was no response.

What is all this, thought Taam, *the gryphon and now my sister talking to me in my own head? I feel so used, so violated. I have no control over the conversation. What thoughts do they hear? How can I guard my thoughts?* Taam pondered these things for a long while and finally resolved to speak to Loy about it.

Taam went over and picked up the gold bands lying in the sand. They were cold to the touch. He thought they would have gotten at least warm in the sun. They were three fingers wide with scroll work etching along the edges. The finish was smooth and craftsmanship of the highest quality was evident. They hinged on one side, but there was no clasp or locking mechanism of any kind on the other. He decided to take them with him when he headed for the castle that evening and laid them close by.

XX

Ora

Settling down with the book again, he started on the sixth chapter. It read more like a tale than a guide. It spoke of a girl in her youth and how she lived near a lake of crystal clear water. She, having a gift, could feel the power of the stone. It would sing to her when her mind was relaxed. The songs were about events from the past and of the future. She could see how the two intertwined like roots from two trees, binding each other together, while choking each other out. She called it 'prius exertus quodin' or the war of history pushing into the present. The girl didn't know the old language, but somehow she understood, as if the stone sang to her very core.

The girl would swim in the lake and get as close as she could to the power calling to her. It took many years of practice diving deeper and holding her breath longer to even come close to the bottom of the lake. The deeper she would dive, the heavier the pressure—and sometimes it was harder to go up than down. The light above would be dimmer than the light below, confusing her about which way the surface was. She would stop and relax her body, allow the air in her lungs to assist her ascent, and then push herself in that direction.

As a child, she'd kept her visions to herself. She believed they were caused by madness. Her belief stemmed from the time an old woman in a nearby town went mad. When the old woman's husband died she'd began to see and hear things which were not there. Everyone said she was mad, and eventually she'd died friendless and alone. The girl thought the people's reaction was horrible and the outcome even worse. She vowed to never let that happen to her.

In time, the girl began to notice other things happening, which she simply could not explain. One day, she went to search for honey in the usual way. Beginning in a field of flowers where honey bees were working, she slowly walked around the edge of the field. Honey bees, she knew, flew about ten to twelve cubits above the ground. She focused her vision on that height, eventually seeing the little insects streaking by in a narrow band. Following their trail, finding each turn they made, was the hard part, as honeybees never flew a straight path to their hive. But after some time and with a farmer's patience, she finally found the hive in a hollow of an old ash tree.

As she had many times before, she relaxed her body and her mind to rid herself of the odor of fear or of malice. The bees would react violently to both. In this state she would usually gently climb the tree to the mouth of the hollow and remove a small piece of comb full of honey and place it in the wide mouth vessel strung around her shoulder. All the while she would make a special effort to prevent harm to the overall hive and its inhabitants.

But this time, before she began her climb, the stone began a song, which spoke of a time when she would accomplish tasks with little effort. It spoke of the old language she would learn. The sound of the words in her mind had a rhythm about them, which could not be reproduced by humankind. It was like the beating of bird's wings or the swishing tails of fish, maybe even the rustling of the leaves as the wind slides through them. The sound inside her head filled her up, as if a light illuminated her from the inside out. There was no darkness in her anywhere.

When she opened her eyes, she realized that hours had passed. Her honey jar was full. Her mind felt overwhelmed, as if she had obtained a lifetime of information in one day. She placed her hand on the tree and felt its power. She knew it had been witness to the arrival of the stone.

After that time, unexplained occurrences such as that began happening more often. She knew this wasn't madness. The stone in the bottom of the lake had let her know without doubt.

By the time she was fourteen, she was finally able to reach the lake bottom. She would grope through the mud on the bottom searching for the stone. She searched for weeks until, eventually, she found it. Although it was the size of a cantaloupe, the stone wasn't heavy. It was a dull grey and very porous. After cleansing it, she saw that it was covered with fractures. She worked the fractures with her fingers, until they eventually gave way to cracks. These allowed her to slip in her fingers and open the stone the whole way.

When the stone gave way and the two halves rested in her hands, she caught a glimpse of the gemstone inside. It was the darkest purple she had ever seen. The preview lasted for but a moment and then everything went black. It was as if the gem took in a breath of light, a gasp. It took in all the light at one time. It was the darkest dark she had ever experienced—and it terrified her.

But the darkness lasted a very short time and the light returning made her eyes water. When she focused on the gem again it had turned to a clear blue. It throbbed with power. She could *feel* the power within it, and it made the hair on her arms stand on end. It was so beautiful, she thought.

She carefully picked it up out of the husk, which now crumbled at her touch. The gem was transparent and drew her interest immediately. Holding it up above, her she peered through the gem as if looking through a lens. She looked into the sky, then at a passing cloud, and slowly worked her way down to the horizon. The trees across the lake around the shoreline looked different. She took the jewel down from her eye and looked at the trees across the lake, then looked through it again. Something wasn't the same, but it was hard to tell what it was.

She looked around and saw a very large tree near her. She looked at it through the gem and she could see a difference. It had a power and it was very strong. She moved closer to the tree and looked again, focusing on just one leaf. It was as if she could see the very life force moving through it. The leaf was drinking in the power of the sunlight, and that energy was moving all through the tree. It was growing, moving, and living and she could see it all through the small clear blue stone she held in her hand.

Looking at a smaller, obviously younger tree, it was as if she was just looking through a tinted crystal. The power just wasn't in the younger trees. This seemed strange to her. Why could she see the life force of the larger tree, when the smaller tree looked normal? She went back to the large tree and stood at the base. It was a massive oak with roots bulging from the ground many cubits away, and a thick trunk which would take at least five large men to reach hand in hand around it. She sat on a gnarled root and looked at the tree for a long time.

"I wish you could talk," she said finally.

She sat wondering and looking until a slight breeze rustled the leaves over her head. The rustling continued on and she closed her eyes and listened. The whispering of the leaves finally began to sound like music, or more like a song which had tempo but couldn't be sung by a human voice.

She could hear the words, though. They were more inside her mind than in her ears. It was a language of old. The words didn't make sense at first, but this is what they said:

"Creation, the power."	genero potentiao
To power to life.	potentia vitao
To life the will.	vitao volo
The will to create."	volo genero

"Are you speaking to me?" asked the girl.

I know you.

We know you.

We know who you are and who you will be.

We know what you possess.

You possess the Lumen Lacertosus.

The girl looked down at the gem in her hand. "Is that what you call this?" She held the gem out toward the tree.

You are Ora.

You are the oracle.

You possess the Lumen Lacertosus.

You are Ora.

She looked at the tree, puzzled. "I'm not Ora. That is not my name. You don't know me, you don't know anything!"

Overwhelmed with fear, she turned to run. As she took a couple of steps the roots around her boiled from the ground. They tripped her and caused her to stumble, until she sat facing the tree with a curled root holding her back upright. The words the tree sang were clear in her head now and meanings of the words were unmistakable.

Ora! ...Ora! ...Ora!

You are the oracle.

You possess the Lumen Lacertosus.

You must learn.

You are bound.

We will teach you.

You are bound.

The girl, now understanding that possessing the stone was a responsibility which bound her to a path, accepted the task at hand. She realized that a lot must be learned and adventures of an uncommon nature would surely follow. She would use the new name she'd acquired and start an entirely new life. The trees, through their songs, explained that they were alive when the Lumen Lacertosus had arrived on this world. They explained the meaning of the first song she'd heard, which she named in the book, *The Song of the Circle of Creation*.

The first line, *The creation, the power*, referred to the origin of all power. When a world was created, the power of the creation lived on in the world. All life came from that power, hence the second line, *To power to life*. The third line pertained specifically to creatures of human-like reasoning. The first beings of this world that fit this description were the Elves. Elves, unlike their human successors, were very adept at manipulating the power. *To life the will* referred to those beings' ability to manipulate the power. There was an important limit placed on the gift, as stated in the last line. *The will to create* would require that the power to manipulate must be for the purpose of creation.

Creation moved power from one place to another or stored the power for later use. The sun as the primary source of power was consumed by a plant—creation. The plant was eaten by an insect or an animal, grew and reproduced—this too was creation. After the creature procreated, passed waste, or its body died and was consumed by other living things and they procreated, the process of creation continued. The power itself continued on. It was never consumed in a way that it couldn't be built upon again. It is possible for power to be consumed in a way that it could no longer be usable. When power was used to destroy something, the power within the object and the power used to destroy it might cease to exist.

The lives touched by the Lumen Lacertosus obtained a mixture of power from this world and from the place the stone originated. The gem had brought into this world an unrelated power, which defied the rules of the world. That is why the trees which were of the old world could think as well as communicate, and other creatures were able to achieve certain capabilities. The creatures of long life were unicorns—they were the most powerful. Dragons were oldest, but few were left. Gryphon, who were the guardians of the kings. Elves, which were all gone and Dwarfs which were in hiding and few creatures knew where.

XXI

The Elder

Taam had been so engrossed in the book, that the sound of approaching people failed to register until, suddenly, he could hear the words of their chant. Quickly, he thought the words of concealment, remembering to hide the tracks made by him and the gryphon. Everything faded from sight except the two gold cuffs still lying nearby. With his heart almost beating out of his chest, Taam spoke feverishly all the words he knew in the old language to conceal them. He felt that the power was being manipulated by the clerics to allow them to be found therefore finding the gryphon. Using the Lumen Lacertosus, he spoke the words again, and the combined power made the cuffs fade into concealment just as the column of clerics topped the dune in front of him.

They were chanting in a language similar to the old one. Taam tried to translate loosely: "Bring us to our lost prize; bring our lost prize to us." The cleric in the lead held a twig in his hands. It was forked and he held one branch in each hand with the base of the twig pointing the way. Upon arriving at the top of the dune the branch fell limp, no longer pointing the way, and the column stopped. The lead cleric looked puzzled and shook the branch as if to try and wake it.

The others gathered around, each one speaking words from their twisted language trying to revive their search. From what Taam overheard, they didn't know what to do. They were very afraid of the reaction they would get from their master, Mach. This name was familiar to Taam, and it took a while before he remembered the class on recent events. Mach was the leader of the clerics. If he was with the soldiers, then the search for the castle must be very important.

Mach must have been holding the gryphon captive using the gold cuffs. I can't imagine how they put them on her, as fierce as she is, thought Taam.

The clerics, having lost their prey, were now moving away, arguing amongst themselves about who was going to tell Mach of their failure. Taam released the power which obscured him and sighed deeply.

You've done well, boy, said the strong female voice in his head. "I've enjoyed Ora's experiences, too."

I do not appreciate the intrusion, thought Taam. You are not welcome to listen to my thoughts at will.

I see, responded the gryphon. I do not intrude, boy, you just think loudly. I can't help but overhear you. She laughed a robust laugh, as if the statement was hilarious.

Are you taunting me, gryphon, after I have freed you from your captors? Taam had made the thought sound loud to himself. But to his surprise, she had no reply. He then spoke aloud. "I said, are you taunting me, beast?"

Beast? You call me a beast? You who must speak with the very organ he eats with? You best have kind words, boy. You wouldn't want anything in your mouth you wouldn't want to swallow.

Taam sat quietly for a while not knowing what to say. He thought she seemed very combative for one who had just gained her freedom.

Maybe she needs something else, something to gain her respect. Respect, that's what is missing... He thought of something his father told him long ago: "Son, how can you gain the respect of a stranger? First you must get to know the person, and you must show respect to gain respect."

Taam said out loud, "My name is Taam. What name would you have me address you by?"

Presida the protector, replied the gryphon.

"Well, Presida, how was such a powerful and wise creature as you captured by the clerics?" asked Taam.

Ah, boy, you are capable of learning, aren't you, she said. I'll tell you my story if you will complete the story you were reading. I would love to hear how it turns out.

Taam thought about it and agreed. Presida scurried over the dune behind him and curled up at his feet. *May I listen through your thoughts?* she asked. *It is much more vivid that way.*

Taam sighed. "Alright, just this time... and thank you for asking." Picking up the book again he began, to read.

Ora had left her home by the lake soon thereafter and traveled to a mountainous region. She'd been instructed to find the oldest tree in the land, within a shallow valley, on the side of a mountain. Along the way, she found trees that had been gifted by the stone, and communicated with them.

"Trees are not unlike people," she said, "they have personalities and culture and some won't talk to people at all."

She saw a dragon along the way, but the dragon had seen her first and disappeared over the horizon before she was able to call out. She'd written that it moved in such a graceful manner, what a beautiful creature it was.

Eventually, she did find the valley. From the edge of a cliff she could see the woods below. It was a very old wood, indeed. When she looked through the gem, almost the entire wood was glowing with the power of the ancient trees.

I hope they all don't sing at once—it might be deafening, she thought.

Down on the valley floor, she found the ground beneath the tall trees had no grass. There was a soft yellow moss covering the earth, with an occasional root stump rising up then curling down.

She walked through the wood, awed by the majesty around her. She could feel the trees' power as much as she felt them watching her. She heard not a sound. There were no birds or insects, not even a rustling of leaves. She had walked for nearly half an hour when she heard a very quiet whisper.

"Left… left…"

She turned left and continued walking, until she heard another guiding whisper.

"Right… right…"

She continued right until she came to a huge wall of gnarled bark. It sloped up in front of her at an angle she could almost walk up, until far over her head it became vertical.

"This isn't a wall… this is a tree. A tree such as I've never seen before!" said Ora.

The tree was so tall that the leaves on the first branches were only a distant blur. She couldn't even tell what kind of tree it was.

"Are you the eldest tree?" she asked. There was no response. She asked the other trees nearby if this was the oldest tree. None of them responded. Eventually, she made her camp for the night, wrapping herself in the moss for warmth, and slept until morning.

Ora awoke to a sound nearby. It sounded like footsteps, but they weren't human. Whatever it was, it had four feet. Even though it was well into the morning, the canopy overhead blocked out the light, making it feel very early. Without moving, she looked for what was making the noise. The darkness made it difficult to see, but she caught a glimpse of white passing between the trees. It wasn't a quick or stealthy movement.

As she watched between the trees where she thought it should appear next, her heart beat rapidly. Then, she saw a shadow of what looked like the shaft of a spear. Next, a head—the white head of a horse appeared in the dark space between the trees. The horse stopped, its entire front quarter exposed to her. Ora sat up, wide-eyed with the realization that there was no spear. It was a long twisted horn protruding from the beast's head. It was a graceful-looking animal with a beauty all its own.

"It's a unicorn!" breathed Ora.

The clean white shape moved with a grace that only the most elegant of creatures possessed. Moving slowly, the magnificent stallion stopped only steps from Ora and gazed into her eyes.

With a voice as handsome as the unicorn's essence, he spoke to her through his thoughts. *You have come to seek council from the Elder?*

Ora bowed her head. "Yes, Ulterius."

You honor me, young one. What do you seek? said the unicorn.

Ora raised her eyes. "I was told to learn from the oldest tree, for I am bound by the possession of the Lumen Lacertosus to do so."

The unicorn seemed to smile, as much as his face would allow, and said, "My dear young human, show me this prize you claim."

Ora took the gem out of her wraps and held it out in her open hand. The unicorn looked up at the giant tree then back down at her as if he had spoken with the tree. He turned and walked away from her, and disappeared in the woods.

Ora was dumbstruck as she watched the animal walk away. "What do I do?" she yelled.

A deep voice answered her. This voice was the Elder and there was no mistaking it. She could feel the voice as much as hear it in her mind. *For what question do you seek the answer?*

"I have many, Master Elder," said Ora, "but first, why did the trees at the lake give me the name Ora?"

"The word 'ora,' is of the old language," he began, "and it means 'region.' The Elves had another meaning when it was used as a name—it reflected the person as a place holder in time. The region you possess is a portion of time. You will be spoken about, written about, and remembered as a marker of an era. Perhaps one would say: 'In the time of Ora, the unicorns still grazed along the Euphrates.'"

"Master Elder, you do not sing your words, you speak clearly and I understand you. Why do the other trees of gifted abilities not do the same?" asked Ora.

"Young one, you honored the unicorn with a title—Ulterius. That title truly belongs to me, for I am more advanced than any other."

Ora spoke to the Elder for months. The unicorn brought food and the stream nearby quenched her thirst. She slept at the foot of her teacher and he protected her from the elements. The knowledge she obtained was timeless and irreplaceable. At the foot of her master she grew to become a young woman, and with the care of a unicorn she knew what the beauty of the world truly was for they taught her all she needed to be great. She came to understand the words of the old language, and the responsibility that knowledge carried with it.

But there was another gift that the stone would give Ora.

On the day she went out into the world the ancient one said, "Young one, as long as you carry this stone, you will not grow old, or be ill. The power it carries is not like the power of this world—it will renew you and nurture you as in your prime. When you no longer carry the stone, this power will no longer be with you. You will be as any other human."

Taam closed the book and looked at Presida. He pulled the gem from the spine of the book and pocketed them both.

"That was the end of the tale," he said aloud. "What is your story?"

XXII

Presida

Presida pushed up with her front legs, and stretched her back in a catlike movement. She turned her head, twisting her neck and stretching it out until all the feathers stood out on ends. She yawned and moved her shoulders around, making sinews pop over her muscular shoulders. *Don't you think you should be getting on your way to the lost city?* she finally said.

Presida trotted up the dune, where the clerics had been. She used her outstretched wings to assist her movement up the shifting sand. After standing for a moment looking out at the sandy wasteland, she turned and walked sideways back down the hill to keep her balance.

Taam still sat, knees tucked under his chin, his arms wrapped around his shins. "Presida, are you going to keep your end of the bargain?" he asked.

She looked at him, yet her face had the same expression it always had.

A beak tends to make it hard to smile or frown, thought Taam. It is very difficult to read the language of a face with no expression.

The gryphon sat down on her haunches nearby and picked her front foot up, carefully examining her talons. I am not nearly as old as the Eldest Tree, or even the noble unicorn which resides in those woods. I found my honor in the service of kings. I am from a time after the Elves. When humans became more civil than not, they recognized fellow humans as their kings. Usually the kings were wiser than their minions and recognized the need for council.

She rose and shook her coat, causing a light fog of sand to escape from her fur and feathers. Relaxing on her other haunch, she began again.

The first human king came to the cave of a gryphon. He was going to kill it, and the trophy would stand as evidence of his power. No one would question his authority if he succeeded, for no man had dared to attack a gryphon. At that time we could not communicate with humans, as the Lumen Lacertosus had not arrived. The gryphon that lived in the cave was wise though, and understood what the human's goal was. Her name was Sis, and she was willing to try to communicate with the human king.

Sis waited for the man to travel deep into her lair and caught him with no fight at all. The man was stricken with fear, as he had no idea that she was so clever. He babbled on for hours while Sis listened intently. He used spoken words and gestured with his hands. He even drew pictures in the sand, trying to communicate to her that he'd leave and never come back.

Seeing how he attempted to communicate gave her an idea of how to talk to this man. Through gestures and drawings in the sand, she began talking with him. They came to an agreement to work together for the benefit of both man and beast. She would allow him to claim victory over her, but she would be his personal guard and council in private. In essence, a truce was brokered and they both profited from the deal.

Over the centuries, up until the Proles began training the sons of the kings, a new gryphon has served each new king. After the Lumen Lacertosus, gryphon could hear the thoughts of the ones they served. But this was bad for both parties involved. The humans had thoughts which offended us, and the kings felt insecure knowing they had no secrets from their guardians.

The kings took the last advice of the gryphon and forged a relationship with the Proles. The gryphon then used their new found abilities and concealed themselves from man. That's the story of the gryphon and the kings. Presida got up and began to walk away.

"Where are you going?" said Taam. "That isn't your entire story. Where are you going?" He stood, picked up the gold cuffs, and began following her.

You know Mach has abilities that exceed those of many common humans, don't you? asked Presida.

"How do you mean?" said Taam.

He knows things that he shouldn't know. He would never let me see exactly what he knew and he stayed far enough away that I couldn't see his thoughts, she said.

"There is a limit on how far you can hear thoughts?" said Taam as he struggled up a dune. "Why can I hear my sister within my mind while we are so far apart?"

I heard your sister in your mind. She is using a conduit to communicate with you. There are still many old trees and creatures alive, which were here at the arrival. The Proles have used this method for a long time. Sha uses an object to communicate through another object and through another, until a conduit is created that will allow energy to flow both ways between two people. Both humans must be Proles, and both must know how it is done.

"But *I* don't know how it's done," said Taam.

Did you not understand what you read? asked Presida. You have the Lumen Lacertosus; it is a power from a different world. It isn't more powerful, just different. Wherever it came from, all living things think with reason and communicate with their minds, I assume. Its arrival changed this world forever.

They walked on for a league without speaking. Taam tried to imagine what exactly in his life had been touched by the gem in his pocket. He wondered if it would be better if the gem was destroyed.

"What would happen, Presida, if the Lumen Lacertosus was destroyed?"

The gryphon stopped in her tracks and spun her head all the way around to look at him, as an owl would do. She didn't answer, eventually turning back and moving forward.

That is an interesting question, she said finally. I'm not sure what would happen—either to the creatures affected by it, or to the place in which it was destroyed... In fact, I can't imagine how one could destroy it.

"Loy, my teacher, taught me how important balance is," said Taam. "It seems this stone has thrown the entire world out of balance. If balance isn't restored, it could be a disaster."

Is the gem what Mach wants? thought Taam. *Is it the power of the stone he seeks? That could change everything.* He could see in his mind all the worlds colliding during his stay at Arborludusium. Even though it was a representation, it did seem very real. It seemed hard to imagine that a small stone could cause so much trouble.

They walked quietly for another hour.

"You still haven't told me how you were captured by Mach," he said.

They topped a dune and the silhouette of the castle rose up out of the sand ahead. The sun was setting and it would soon be dark.

Presida moved close to Taam and looked at him eye-to-eye. You have much to do. You should speak to this Ora, if you can find her. I don't know where the Elder tree is, but she does. The Elder seems the ultimate authority on the balance, as you say. I am leaving now and may not return. The gryphon turned and, with the fury of a procella, she was gone.

Upon Taam's arrival at the gate, which now had guards posted on the towers, Master Vele called down to him. He held up his hand to signal back and sank to his knees with exhaustion. As the doors opened and Loy come in to view, Taam closed his eyes. He felt the sand rise up and embrace his face.

As hands on his arms lifted him from the ground, Taam heard Sha speaking to him in his mind. Her voice echoed as though the sound came from within a well. This time he didn't speak out loud. The words soon became clearer, as if she rose to the top of the well.

Taam, she said, what are you doing? I only see darkness.

I'm sleeping, said Taam. Why are you invading my mind? How are you invading my mind?

I'm not invading. She sounded annoyed. I'm just speaking to my brother. Don't you care about your family anymore?

Well of course I care, thought Taam. What has happened?

Much, said Sha. Mother and I have wands from an old holly tree and we can do things with them. We're staying with Loy's father because soldiers came by the farm. I saw the gryphon—did it hurt you?

No, not really…I mean not intentionally… well maybe a little—he said.

I'm going to learn to read runes. Josiah's going to teach me! she interrupted.

Sha, stop! You need to stop and listen to me. In his mind he spoke to her face-to-face, his hands grasping both her shoulders. The wand gathers its power from the Lumen Lacertosus. It is not of this world and you should not use it. All your abilities are from this gem. Using the power could damage Mundus Terra and—

Sha interrupted his pleading. No! I'm using it right now to speak to you. I will use it to protect our family, and you can't make me stop!

They both were silent. Sha, he knew, because she was angry that he would take from her what came naturally to him. He was silent because he couldn't make her understand.

Sha, if you use this power, never use it to destroy or hurt anything or anyone. And you need to prepare for a trip, because you and I must travel to the Elder tree.

Sha paused. When will we be leaving?

I'm not sure, but I'll contact you, said Taam. They said their farewells and Taam drifted back to sleep.

When he awoke, he noticed Loy sitting beside him reading a scroll. Without moving his head, Taam looked about the room and slid his hand into his pocket to verify that the gem was still in his possession. Feeling it there gave him a sense of relief, so he sat up in the bed. Pushing himself up caused sharp pains in both shoulders.

Loy was up immediately and helped him to sit. "You need to take care, young man, or you'll open your wounds."

Taam looked around once more but didn't recognize where he was. After Loy had propped him up with pillows, Taam leaned back and relaxed. "Where am I?" he asked.

"You're in my mother's home," replied Loy.

"Good, I'll need to speak to her," said Taam.

"The Council wants to speak to you as soon as you're well enough," said Loy in his authoritative voice.

"I don't have time to wait," said Taam, wincing from a tinge in his shoulder. "I must speak to Ora. Teacher, will you ask her to come?"

Loy nodded and left the room. In a few minutes Loy and Ora both entered.

Ora had a smile on her face. "Ah, you look much better than you did yesterday! I've brought you something to eat." She held up a bowl of soup.

The smell of food made Taam realize he was very hungry. Taking the bowl and thanking her, he began his tale. "When I was standing on the wall looking for the—"

Ora interrupted him. "Taam, you need to tell this tale to the entire Council, not to just me."

"I was told to speak to you," said Taam.

Ora looked puzzled. "By whom?"

"By Presida the protector," he replied. "She said I must ask you where to find the Elder—"

Ora placed a finger on his lips to quiet him. "The walls have ears. Rest now and eat. We will speak later in the council

147

chamber after you regain your strength," she said, looking around at the room. Then she smiled at Taam, placing a finger to her lips to remind him to not speak here.

As Taam continued his meal, he and Loy shared a knowing look.

Taam spent the entire day and night in bed, with Loy tending his wounds and bringing him sustenance as needed. Their talk was insignificant and it bored them both. Their only enjoyment was in their games of chess, which Loy was losing more and more often.

The following morning Taam was up walking around and his wounds were almost healed. Loy showed him what he was using to treat his wounds and explained the methods he used to manipulate power for healing. Master Vele visited with him for a short time before midday and explained that the Council was limiting visitors. They would not allow the twins to visit.

When Loy brought in the midday meal, Taam noticed he also carried his walking staff. When Master Vele had gone, Loy took the staff and laid it across the bed, gesturing to Taam to grasp it. As soon as Taam touched the staff, he heard a presence in his mind.

It was Loy. Taam, don't say a word, just listen for a little while. My father told me your sister was able to contact you. Very few have that gift. We speak to each other through the use of this part of an oak tree.

The fact that the clerics got so close makes us feel that there is someone within the city in contact with Mach. That is why my mother asked you not to speak. Is there something you can speak to me about?

Loy speaking to Taam wasn't the same as Presida speaking to him. Presida had filled his mind, as if her very presence was within him. Loy's speech, on the other hand, felt more like when he talked to his sister. It was more like a conversation than sharing thoughts and feelings. This consideration made Taam understand why the gryphon wanted to listen to the reading within his mind. His feelings would be part of the story to her.

Where are the gold cuffs? thought Taam.

The Council has them, answered Loy. I wouldn't let them touch the stone or the book, though.

Taam nodded in appreciation. I removed them from the gryphon, freeing her from the Mach's bonds. She told me that Mach is powerful, in the way the Proles are. He is also very smart—he stayed away from Presida to prevent her from knowing his thoughts. They were looking for what they call the Lost City. I guess they mean the Inculta Pugnaculum.

Is there anything you want me to pass on to my mother? asked Loy.

Yes, said Taam, I must go to the Edest Tree. She knows where it is. I need to take my sister with me. The council of the tree will help me to understand how to obtain balance.

Loy smiled. "I see you've learned your lessons well." He picked up Taam's empty bowl and mug and left the room.

XXIII

Veneficus

Josiah sat reading the scroll in his lap with Sha at his feet. As he read story after story, she drank them in as if driven by thirst. Every once in a while, some of the old language was used in the stories; Sha hid the information in the back of her mind for later use. She was very careful when asking questions to prevent Josiah from knowing what she was learning. She learned words like: 'excessum,' meaning death; 'evinco,' meaning defeat; 'noceo,' to do harm; 'extractum,' meaning to remove; and finally 'obruo,' meaning to destroy.

"You know, I used to read to Loy in this very place," said Josiah. "He used to love the stories of the Elves. Of course, they were a very wise and creative people. Most of the forests were planted by the Elves you know. Well, the old ones. The younger forests were mostly started by the Proles or grew naturally. I wish I could have met one—an Elf, I mean. They were gone well before I was born. Now Ora, she met one. She said they were elegant people and they loved to sing and dance, or was that the Dwarfs? I don't remember."

"Do you still have writings of the Elves?" asked Sha.

"Yes, my dear, but it wouldn't do you any good to hear one, for they are written in the old language."

150

Sha's eyes brightened. "That's alright; I would like to hear it in the old language. I think it would sound like music or a poem."

Josiah thought about it for a moment. "It would be good to hear if you're learning the old language. If the Council says that you should learn, then I'll not only read them to you, but I'll teach you to read them yourself. They were left here to help the humans advance when they are deemed ready."

"You mean when we're ready," she said.

"My," said Josiah, "you are quite a student, aren't you. Yes I mean when *we* are ready."

After Josiah read some more to her and she'd completed some chores, Sha ventured out away from the house looking for the old trees. None of the trees she found sang to her like the giant holly had, but she could feel something from some of them. She leaned against those trees, her back pressed against the trunk, relaxing her mind and body. Warmth emanated from them and into her. She felt a power deep within the trees, the old ones, a physical connection she couldn't describe. She longed to feel what the holly tree had shared with her, and she couldn't understand why she couldn't get that back.

Her earlier conversation with her brother, though it angered her, still resonated in her mind. Why should she not practice the gift?

What is it that I don't know? What about this Elder tree, is it like the holly tree? What do I need to do to get ready for this trip? When are we going? Another tree perhaps, another tree would know. She continued searching.

Josiah and Hym were discussing a method of thwarting insects from cabbage when Hym's wife leaned out of the back door, waving to attract the two men's attention. She motioned for them come to the door. "There are people in the front," she told them.

Josiah passed through the house and opened the door to two tall men entering the front gate. He closed the door behind him and spoke to the men for some time. Hym and his wife could not hear the conversation. He came back in and quickly gathered a fresh loaf of bread and a small container of an herb and went back out to the visitors. Re-entering the house he turned and stood in the doorway, watching as the two men left.

"Please go and gather your daughter to us," he said. "We need to depart from this house. The two men have delivered a warning that the soldiers will be arriving here tomorrow. Hym, please assist me in moving the library as they will surely destroy it."

Hym followed Josiah's lead, gathering the tablets, while his wife went to find their daughter.

Sha had abandoned her search. She was far enough away from the house to see the two men leaving, yet remain unseen by them. She sat hidden in her place until her mother came out searching for her. When she approached, Sha came out to meet her and asked about the two men.

"They brought news to Josiah that the soldiers will be coming tomorrow. We need to prepare to leave," replied her mother.

Sha reached into her waist belt, pulling out the holly wand, and pointed down the road in the direction the men had come. "I'm ready for them!" she said.

Her mother placed her hand on Sha's. "We're ready for them, dear." They smiled at each other and went back to the house.

Josiah and Hym carried the entire library into a dug out floor space in the tool shed, along with the silver and gold utensils, and then replaced the floorboards over them. Their bundles and bags were packed with dried goods and essentials and stacked outside. Josiah removed the acorn from the transom and hid it in the woods in a hollow tree. He showed all three where it was, so Loy could be informed if anything happened to Josiah.

About three hours before sunset, they began their journey. Since they'd received no answer from Loy, they headed in the direction of the Inculta Pugnaculum.

Josaih talked as they walked, "I've been there many times with my wife. I never wanted to live there though. I always told her too many people live there. I don't know how you can think with all that activity."

They made excellent time, since Josiah knew the way and took advantage of every short cut available to them. He knew the trip would take a couple of weeks, but it didn't dampen his spirit at all. He knew he would be passing by an oak tree in three days which would allow some communication with his son. He also took great care to leave no trail for the soldiers follow.

Shortly before darkness fell, they made camp on a small knoll overlooking the path they'd just traveled. They made no fire, so the soldiers following would have no evidence of their location. Josiah collected some young sprigs of tasty greens, common in the area during early spring. "The more food we forage, the less of our provisions we'll use," he told them.

As they lay back in the evening, Josiah spoke of old Elvish tales and adventures. He told how they navigated the world using the stars. He said that stars' lifespans were so great, landmarks would come and go, but the stars never moved.

Sha dreamed of Elves and stars and battling the soilders with her mother, their wands in hand. One vivid dream was of her standing on a rise with the wind at her back. Her hair was blowing out around her head, obscuring her vision. Her mother was just below her on the rise, coming up with fear in her eyes and tears on her cheeks. Sha pushed her hair aside and saw that several soldiers were just behind her mother. One of the soldiers stopped and nocked an arrow in his bow.

Just then, her mother's face turned cold and hard with anger, for she had just seen the fear in Sha's eyes. She turned and pulled her wand from her sleeve and pointed it at the group. The sound of the word "Ignis!" resonated in the valley and rebounded as an echo, deep and loud. The valley became a blazing inferno.

An arrow flew past her mother. It was in on fire and stuck in the trunk of a tree near Sha.

Sha awoke in a cold sweat. The morning was just beginning and the light was just enough to see that the camp was empty except for her. She bit her lip to make sure she wasn't still dreaming. Realizing that this was no dream, she got up and walked to the edge of the rise. As she looked down the hill a wind came up, blowing her hair in her eyes. Her blood ran cold as her dream came true before her eyes.

She fell to the ground sobbing.

XXIV

Oak

Sha finally stood and looked at what was left of her dream. The ground was scorched as far as she could see from where her had mother stood. Not even her mother survived the fire produced by her own anger. She'd been consumed by the very power she manipulated. As Sha walked down the hill, she counted the soldiers, who would only be identifiable by their brass and copper armaments. There were forty-seven. She wondered where her father and Josiah were.

She wandered to the bottom of the valley to the small stream and washed the tears from her face. Her grief surged; she couldn't stop crying. She got up and walked upstream, where she found Josiah. He lay upon his face, an arrow rising up from his back just above a kidney. She fell to her knees beside him and pushed him onto his side. He was still alive and tears began to fall from Sha's eyes once more.

He spoke to her with a great deal of pain in his voice. "Sha, hand me your wand." She took it out of her waistband and handed it to him. "Hold the end," he said. She held onto it and they both held the wand for a few moments. When Sha closed her eyes to blink away more tears, she saw Josiah standing in her mind. But when she opened her eyes, they were still both on the ground holding her wand.

She closed her eyes again and Josiah smiled at her. Sha, he said, we are in my mind because I have much to say, but very little time to spend with you. Listen to me first and, if there is time, I'll answer any questions you have.

Sha nodded.

Your father and I saw the camp from the knoll, he continued. They must have come to the house early. Hym and I went down to scout and count their numbers, when we noticed your mother had followed us. I went back to get your mother out of sight when a patrol found your father. When they struck him down, your mother screamed. I was next, and I don't know what happened to your mother.

Sha relayed to him what had happened and the fact that she had dreamed the event before it occurred.

Do not continue on this way, Josiah told her. *No one will know you even exist. This is what you must do.* He took her hand in her mind and began to fly. They flew up the hill, but it was not scorched at all. They flew on hand-in-hand as he showed her the path to the oak tree. There they stopped. He described in detail how to contact Loy at the Inculta Pugnaculum. *What questions do you have?*

"Why was the hill not scorched?" said Sha.

"I have not seen the hill scorched; you see it here as I have seen it in the past," he answered.

Why did the fire consume my mother?"

Josiah's face lost any happiness it might have had. The power she used was destructive, not constructive. It was probably manipulated in anger, and her reaction was not thoroughly thought out. This is what a veneficus does, and unfortunately her name will be removed from every record and every mind. Even her memory will cease to exist. This is why you must be very careful in how you use the power you have obtained.

Josiah began to fade from Sha's mind. I have to leave you, Sha. When you see my wife and son, please share this memory with them so they know I love them both and my last thoughts are of—.

He was gone. She opened her eyes to see Josiah was no longer breathing, but a smile was on his face. She rose and went to the top of the hill. And as she past the place where her mother had stood, she didn't even notice it for the memory of the veneficus had already faded.

She collected the items she needed and consolidated them into one heavy pack. She took the three statuettes of her, her father, and her brother and placed them in the small leather pouch which hung around her neck. Then she made the camp look as though only two people had slept there and moved toward the place that Josiah had shown her. She moved slowly and carefully, for she was young, scared, and alone. She kept her wand in her hand almost constantly and made herself disapear if she heard a sound or saw a movement.

At night she burrowed into thorny thickets and the made herself invisible. She woke at the slightest sound. When her sorrow filled her up at the loss of her father, she cried silently.

On the third day, she arrived at the oak tree. It was a mighty burr oak with boughs the thickness of a cow's body. She fell against the tree and held onto it as if it were a long lost friend. She felt the warmth radiating from it and into her, making her feel better almost immediately. She reached for the lowest branch and had soon climbed high into the tree, where she found a cradling set of limbs and settled in for the night.

As she slept a restful sleep, she dreamt. Loy was calling out to her, "Sha, are you there?"

"Here I am," said Sha. Loy stood on a stone wall and Sha floated down gently and landed in front of him. It was the dusk and the light was fading quickly. Sha looked around. "Isn't this where the great beast took my brother?"

"Yes," said Loy. "He was just there." He pointed near where Sha stood. "He is alright now. He will meet with the Council tomorrow. Why, Sha, have you called me?"

"Your father, Josiah, has asked me to call you," she replied. "He said you must be made aware of what has occured."

Loy stood quiet for a moment. "Why didn't he contact me in the usual way?"

Sha walked to the edge of the wall to hide her tears. "He can't contact you because of the soldiers." She turned and looked back at Loy. "Teacher, they have killed him. They have killed my father, too."

Loy and Sha both looked down, tears running down their cheeks. "Are you alone Sha?" said Loy.

She wiped her tears with her sleeve. "Yes, but I'm alright; the oak has me here safe and I have food and water."

"I'll send someone to fetch you. Do you know how to conceal yourself."

"Yes, Teacher, I can and I'll wait," answered Sha. "I have not mourned my father. Do you think I should start now?"

"Wait for your brother—you must bear the weight of your father's passing together," he said as his image faded away.

Sha awoke in the comforting boughs of the oak tree. She knew that this was no dream. Someone would be coming for her soon.

XXV

Council Meeting

Taam's shoulders had no more pain in them and the strength in his hands was full again. Today he would speak to the Council. He couldn't understand the distrust in the Council. *For such an advanced group of people, they certainly keep a lot of secrets*, he thought. *Father taught me to trust the family and I have begun thinking of Loy and Master Vele as family. What is it that they all fear so much? What is happening that I know not?*

Loy entered the room, looking as though he'd been up all night. He had his staff in hand and motioned for Taam to come with him. He silently placed something into Taam's hand. It was a small, egg-shaped wood carving with runes on it. Taam recognized the word 'defero,' which meant 'to communicate.'

It must have been carved from the same wood as Loy's staff, he thought. He relaxed a bit and looked for the tunnel in his mind where Loy would be waiting. Keeping an eye on where he was walking and looking for Loy at the same time proved to be a challenge. He found Loy with his back to him, looking off the roof of the Arborludusium. The weather was odd with a dark threatening sky. Loy didn't turn around; he just greeted him with, "Taam."

"Teacher," replied Taam, "are we going to the council chambers?"

Loy sighed heavily. "Yes Taam, but I have something to speak to you about. It seems our lives have twisted together, making us brothers. Both our fathers fell in battle."

Taam stopped walking and his mind brought him to reality where he focused on Loy's face in the hallway—it was hard and expressionless. Taam said nothing aloud, but turned and began walking again. Moving back through the tunnel to Loy's image in his mind, he asked. "What happened?"

Loy's image turned showing all the emotion he was hiding on the outside. "Sha contacted me in a dream. We didn't go into any detail, as it was not the time. She is at my family's oak, waiting for a guide. The question is where is she to go? I cannot answer that without knowing what you're going to tell the Council."

"Is Sha alright?"

"Yes, she is strong for one so young, and the oak will protect her along with her holly wand," answered Loy.

If only I could ask Presida to go and get her, then I know she would be safe, thought Taam.

Taam placed his hands on his hips and heaved an exasperated sigh. "Teacher, I don't have enough information to know exactly what to say, but I do know the result I want."

Loy's image stood silent.

"I need the Council to maintain their position and I need to meet my sister at the eldest tree," said Taam. "I need your mother to take me there. I'll grieve on the way and learn what I need to know upon my arrival."

"Tell them as much of the truth as you can," said Loy, "yet hold back what you think will cause harm to anyone or anything. My mother is the oldest of them all and they all look to her for some guidance. Speak to Procer Gabrel and allow him to lead the conversation. I think you'll do just fine."

Their images faded and Taam turned his attention to their surroundings. He had lost track of where he'd walked and knew he would not find his way back alone. He knew they had left one building and entered another. All the long hallways seemed to look the same, just door after door, seeming to go on forever. They entered a mergence of four halls into a small alcove with a circular bench in the center and a skylight above. The twins were sitting on the bench with Master Vele and a young man Taam did not recognize. The girls saw him, leapt from their places, and ran to meet him.

"Taam, Taam, how are you? They wouldn't let us see you! Are you hurt?"

Taam was flattered—and embarrassed—to be so popular. "I'm alright," he said. "I missed you, too. I'll see you ladies after this encounter with the Council."

Master Vele settled the girls back down; Loy placed a hand on Taam's shoulder and guided him down toward the chamber.

This hall was more familiar. There were sounds, like a crowd of people, coming from up ahead. The double doors were open and pegged in place. Guards stood in the doorway with wooden poles as long as they were tall. Loy and Taam stood in front of the soldiers and waited.

Taam heard Tod over the crowd. "Taam, son of Hym and wielder of the Lumen Lacertosus."

The chamber hushed immediately, and the two guards stepped aside, making room for them to pass. They stepped through the door together and Loy whispered to Taam, "Go on and stand before the Council." Loy went into the crowd.

Taam slowly walked toward the Council. A large group of people were present and he could see them in his peripheral vision. They were mostly older people, and Taam thought they must be the elders of the city. The elders of his town would gather for discussion when there was a threat to the population or something was affecting the entire town.

Suddenly, he realized what was going on. When Presida had grasped his shoulders, he'd been able to see her, but no one else had.

They probably want to know why I flew off the castle wall screaming. Was it Mach? Was it the soldiers? Was it some kind of weapon?

Taam couldn't imagine what these people must have seen. He stopped before the council and bowed low to them, showing them as much respect as he could.

Rising up, Procer Gabrel began. "This council recognizes Taam, welcomes you, and thanks you for your audience. We would like to understand the events of this battle of the gryphon."

Taam bowed again but not as low this time. "I am at your service Procer Gabrel."

"Fine," said Gabrel, "Would you describe this creature you so valiantly slaughtered?"

Taam was surprised by this question and thought – It seems he is trying to lead my answer. He's afraid of the crowd.

"If it pleases the Council, Procer, it would be simpler if I tell the entire tale so no part is left out."

Procer Gabrel shifted in his seat. He glanced over at Ora, who smiled at him. "That would please the Council," he said.

"Early in the morning while on the wall, my teacher and I saw the encampment a half league away. Using the Lumen Lacertosus, I searched the camp for the use of magic, of which I found only one instance. A female gryphon was being held captive by the clerics. She was a graceful creature with feathers and fur and she was very old, indeed. She was concealed from our sight by the cleric Mach. It appears he didn't want to rouse the soldier's suspicions. After warning the Council of the soldiers' presence, I went to the stable as my teacher had instructed me. Then I realized that the Lumen Lacertosus might assist in the search for the gryphon since the soldiers were now on the move.

"Upon my arrival on the wall, the gryphon caught me by surprise, as I had not retrieved the Lumen Lacertosus from its place. She carried me far away from the Inculta Pugnaculum before we stopped in the wasteland. Her talons pierced me though... I don't think she meant to hurt me, for she did not attack me further or try to harm me in any way. I saw the bands of

165

bondage on her legs, and with the power of the Lumen Lacertosus, I removed her bonds to prevent the clerics from using this old creature against anyone."

With this Taam could see a light of contentment in the eyes of Procer Gabrel. Ora too had a smile but Andraya scowled. It was obvious that she did not agree with the others.

"So where is this old decrepit beast?" asked Procer Gabrel.

"She is gone, Procer, across the desert. She flew as fast as she could as if she might be running from captors."

The crowd seemed to relax at this. They began whispering amongst themselves about how they could now let the livestock graze again and their children play outdoors.

Taam spoke up once more. "If it pleases the Council." He bowed again.

"Speak," said Procer Gabrel.

"Procer, I would like to continue my training as soon as possible, as I require a better understanding of the world."

Procer Gabrel looked at all the members of the Council in turn. Each one nodded to him and some spoke quietly agreeing with the need to continue Taam's training.

When he came to Ora, she said, "I think it necessary that I observe some of Taam's training myself. I shall take leave and do so for a while."

At this Gabrel looked at each member again, receiving nods from everyone except Andraya—she did not respond in any way.

"We conclude this council finding no threat," said Procer Gabrel, "and allow Taam's training to continue."

XXVI

Family

The evening meal was more like a feast than just another meal. Taam, Loy, Ora, the twins, all sat at the table. There was also the young man from under the skylight who Taam had not met—he sat between the two girls and directly across from Taam. The meal was held in the garden of Ora's house and all stood around the table until she had seated herself.

Delane introduced the young man to Taam. "This is Culm, we met him while sparing."

Taam introduced himself but had a disconcerting feeling about Culm. He wasn't sure if it was jealousy or if it was instinct. Culm threw out compliments to everyone. It seemed to flatter the girls, but it annoyed Taam. As too much water would drown a plant, too many compliments would turn a head away. The quantity of complements given seemed to drown everyone around him. Culm was attending class with another teacher here in the castle. He did seem to have a good knowledge of the language and he didn't brag. This made Taam feel more comfortable, but he didn't let his guard down.

Taam wanted to discuss his expedition to the eldest tree with Ora, but the past few days had made him very cautious of where he was when he spoke and of who might be listening. He also wanted to speak to Sha about the death of their father. The carved piece of oak was still in his pocket and he thought about talking to Loy while they were at the meal.

How would I have two conversations at one time? he thought. What would happen if he answered someone else with a statement meant for Loy's ears? This could get complicated, so he left it alone.

Finally the end of the evening drew close and the guests excused themselves. Culm walked the twins to their quarters. Loy was tending a chore for his mother and the table was being cleared by Sean. Taam asked Ora if there was a place they could speak. She took him to the edge of the garden near where a couple of sheep were staked.

"Ora, will you take my sister and me to the eldest tree?"

Ora looked at him with tired eyes. "Taam, your sister will meet us there. In fact she will be there long before we arrive. You have dispatched Presida to fetch her, and I have told Presida where to take her."

"I thought Presida was returning to her home," said Taam.

"She has no home to return to. She is a protector of kings. When they decide to become a protector, the rest of their kind banishes them. Though it is a noble undertaking for them, they have to present themselves as defeated by whichever king they serve. The gryphon is one of the mightiest of all creatures since the dragons. They look down on this one act, even though a protector is hailed as a hero among themselves."

"Have you ever met a gryphon?" Taam asked.

"Oh my, yes," said Ora. "I've done a great many things in my life, Taam. Do you know how old I am?"

Taam shook his head, but was thinking she must be at least sixty.

"I'm nine hundred and seventy-two years old. That length of time allows for many leagues traveled and a great many adventures."

Taam's chin hung with surprise.

Ora reached over and pushed his chin up, closing his mouth. "You have freed her from Mach, and for that she will protect you and yours until one of you dies. No one knows that she is around, but she is."

"How long will it take to reach the eldest tree?" Taam asked.

Ora pondered the question for a moment. "I'm not young anymore, dear. I think it will take a little while. We will leave tomorrow, so get some rest and we will speak then. Tonight, use the oak to speak to your sister—let her know that Presida is coming."

Taam bowed to Ora as she left him, and he went to find Loy to guide him to his quarters.

When Taam was quartered for the night, he pulled out the book and placed the gem in its place. The last portion of the book had a list of words. Some were written several times with lines through them, changed a little, then scratched again. The words were different than those of the old language but used the same characters. As Taam thumbed through the book, he noticed that the handwriting was from the same person, but the hand had changed over time.

I wonder if she wrote in this book for over nine hundred years. Taam thought. It looked as if she was trying variations of different words. She may have figured out words that people today do not know. Without knowing their meaning, the words are useless, because one must see it in one's mind first for it to happen.

He removed the stone from the book and placed them in different pockets. Taking the little carved egg in his hand, he relaxed his mind and went searching for his sister. *Defero,* he thought to himself. He saw himself in the great wood that he, Loy, Master Vele, and the twins had passed through. There was no movement of air and it was quiet. He heard only the sound of decaying leaves crunching under his feet.

"Sha," he called out, "are you here? Sha, can you hear me? Defero Sha!"

As Taam walked through the trees calling out to his sister, the sounds of the wood became clearer. The smells, the sounds, everything around him came to life as if he were truly there, only more so.

After a while, and it didn't seem very long, he heard Sha calling back to him. "I'm here, over here!"

When Taam caught sight of her, he thought to himself that she hadn't changed at all. *She looks exactly as I remember her.*

They ran to each other and embraced, both crying for their loss, yet happy to see each other.

"Are you all right?" asked Taam.

Sha only nodded her head yes.

"Can you tell me what happened?" asked Taam.

"We need to see the events in my mind because I don't think I can make it through the tale."

Taam looked at her face to face and nodded to say he was ready.

They held hands and Sha guided him through the trees until they came out onto a small grassy hill. It was dark now; dawn was just about to break. They walked to the spot where the camp was. Sha was sleeping and the other beds were empty. Taam looked behind him and the trees were no longer there. Sha began stirring in her sleep; it was obvious that she was dreaming. She woke up and sat up right in her place. She, too, saw the beds were empty and got up, eventually making her way to the edge of the knoll. The two images of Sha and Taam stood side-by-side, looking down the shallow valley. A woman was running up the hill with several soldiers chasing her.

"Who is that woman?" said Taam.

"I don't know," said Sha.

The woman turned and withdrew a wand and, using the old language, she destroyed all the soldiers with a fire so intense that

Taam and Sha raised their arms to protect themselves from the heat.

"She must be a veneficus; she destroyed that entire army. Where did she go?"

One image of Sha covered her mouth with both hands and gasped in complete surprise; the other looked at the ground in front of her with tears streaming down her face and squeezed Taam's hand. In a little while they all three made their way down the hill to the stream and then to Josiah. They could not hear the conversation which had taken place in Josiah's mind, but Sha did tell Taam that she'd share that information when they were together. She simply could not draw it out of herself without the help of the holly wand.

When they walked to the top of the knoll, the old forest was there again and they went in. They sat for a long time discussing all that had occurred up to now, and especially about Presida coming to take her to the elder tree.

"Be open and honest with all the creatures," said Taam, "including the trees—as they already know what is in your mind."

Taam got up to leave and turning back to his sister, he said, "We shall meet in the woods where the eldest tree stands. There we will learn our fate."

Appendix

Old Language	Current Language	Chapter
aperio	reveal	15
Arborludusium	school of the trees	5
ceno	to dine	5
cubiculum	sleeping room	4
cubit	19 inches	3
defero	to communicate	25
dissimulo	conceal from view	13
equester	cavalry (the knight in chess)	5
evinco	defeat	24
excessum	death	24
extractum	to remove	13
genero	to create	20
honestus	beautiful	17
ignis	ignite flames	7
Inculta Pugnaculum	desert fortress	14
lavatio	wash room	4
league	3.0 statute miles	18
leno	dining room	5
leviter	lightly or weightlessly	6
lingua	language	7
ludusa	school	5
lumen lacertosus	power of the light	11
lunas	a moon	4
memoria	memory	13
Montisludsium	school of the mountains	10
Mundus Rufus	red planet	4

Acknowledgements

The fine line art provided in this edition was created under contract by *Allen Flanigan* of Spring Texas and *Cherylann Case* of Tomball Texas. I thank you both for your excellent work and hope your careers in art flourishes to your liking.

The editing of grammatical works was performed by several people. First my daughter *Shala Geraci,* though it was a burden on her, assisted me greatly in this endeavor. Also my friend *Liz Bello* and her family were instrumental in their assistance in other editing areas along with some very sound advice. I thank you all. Professional editing was performed by *Marlo Garnsworthy*.

Above all I would like to say thank you to my wife for putting up with the eccentricities that seem to go hand in hand with an endeavor such as this.

Coming Soon

The second of this series will soon be here. Watch for "Majik The age of Ora" to be in print in 2010. A host of exciting new adventures will keep you on the edge of your seat. The addition of new characters adds to the exciting turns and twists.

www.ingramcontent.com/pod-product-compliance
Lightning Source LLC
Chambersburg PA
CBHW020441180626
46812CB00003B/1340

To the Love that perpetuates my life

The first day of summer could not have been more beautiful. Angels flew about the vintage garden, giving the air a touch of cool summer breeze that could put a smile on the solemnest of faces. Luckily, not one sad face was among the guests assembled in the chairs—ten chairs across and ten rows back—on each side of the grassy aisle that led to an archway of flowers. Not just any type of flowers, no. There were flesh-toned almond blossoms, bright red clove flowers, lavender forgot-me-not, pink primrose with a purple hue around the edges, globed amaranth and honeysuckles.

The cherubs played the sweetest of melodies from the strings of trees circling the ceremonial spot of love from the past, present, and future. Accompanying them was a symphony of sounds from nature rejoicing, along with the chorus of birds singing harmoniously. The celestial atmosphere for this special occasion was seemingly perfect, with the faint sound of the crashing ocean beating against the cliff below.

This blessed garden is the perfect place for the start of a union.

We could not be happier to see these two humans join

their lives together as one.
One mind, one body, one soul,
and one heart. A holy
unification that is more
powerful as one than any two
could ever be alone.

He follows the Sealer to the
archway. He takes a deep
breath and releases his
reservations about this day
forever and always on the
ocean breeze. The breeze
carries it out beyond the
depth of no return, on the
endless sea of air past the
realm of mortal men. He
turns and looks down the
aisle between the chairs to
the very beginning. He smiles
and becomes feverish with

delight and excitement at what he sees before him.

She is there. More beautiful than visions of her in his dreams, there she stands. He shakes his head ever so slightly, in disbelief that this woman will be his all the days of his life. Her love. Her kisses. Her body. His eyes gravitate to her hips as she moves closer, evoking emotions of erogenous sensations. *Mine*, he thought. *Mine to touch, to hold, and to caress. She will be mine until the end of time.* His smile widens as his thoughts drift to what will come later...not soon enough. He turns to the

Sealer and prays that he will be quick and swift.

She walks down the grassy aisle to meet them both. Her face is covered with a white veil and she holds flowers in both hands, across the waist of her white, flowing gown. She searches his face for any hesitation to her approach. Reassured by what she has found, she walks a half step faster. Her heart pounds harder because of his overt confidence in his decision this day to share his life with her until time itself no longer exists in this world.

She believes in him. She trusts him. She loves him. He

is hers. His love and attention she plans to share with no one – *no one*. If any woman thinks she can tear me from his heart, she has a fight on her hands. He is mine—my protector, my provider, my promoter, my philosopher, and my partner.

She arrives by his side. She hands her flowers to another. He and She stand next to each other in front of the Sealer. The Sealer nods at them. They turn to each other and clasp hands.

I, Zorah Morrison,
take you,
William Hughes

to be my lawfully wedded husband.
To have and to hold from this day forward
To love, cherish, honor and obey
For better or for worse, for richer or poorer, in sickness and in health, to forsake all others til death do us part.
To this I pledge you my solemn vow before God.

I, William Hughes, take you, Zorah Morrison to be my lawfully wedded wife.
To love, cherish, honor and obey

To have and to hold from this
day forward
For better or for worse,
for richer or poorer,
in sickness and in health,
to forsake all others
til death do us part.
To this I pledge you my
solemn vow before God.

The Sealer smiles and
explains that the young
couple want to add to their
vows in unison. William and
Zorah take a breath together
and recite:

Love is patient
Love is kind
It is not envious
It is not boastful
It is not proud or hateful

It does not dishonor others
Or easily provoke them to
anger
It does not rejoice in evil or
sin
But rejoices in the truth
Love bears all things
Love believes in all things
Love hopes in all things
Love endures all things
Love will never fail or end
Our love will never fail us nor
end

They take their rings of
platinum and place them on
each other's hand. The Sealer
places his hand on top of
theirs.

"By the power given to me, I
bless this holy union. Before

these witnesses and God, I pronounce you husband and wife. What God has put together let no man nor beast or spirit put asunder. You may kiss your bride."

William lifts the veil to reveal the full beauty of Zorah. He pulls her close to him and kisses her on the lips with gentle commitment.

The Sealer presents them to the world and the heavens.

"Help me welcome the new couple to the fold of matrimony, William and Zorah Hughes."

The guests rise to their feet, clapping and praising this wonderful alliance within the world. The angels flutter their wings with approval and excitement of the joining of these two souls. The heavens shout and cheer from above with joy and affirmation of this blessing and inspiration of all that is right in the realms of existence.

Well done. Yes, well done, indeed.

So be it.

Chapter 2

The trees around the house are barren without leaves. The house sits at the end of a street, next to a brick wall. Patches of snow cling to the top of brown grass and dry dirt in front of the two-story Victorian brick home. A wooden post, with a "For Sale" sign planted near the mailbox, blows slightly in the frosty wind.

The house is much colder inside than out. All the blinds are drawn up to allow the light that persists to seep through the sky to enter. The luminance chill renders the entire house a pale blue. Even the hardwood floors throughout the entire first floor surrendered their tint to the temperament of the house.

All cabinet doors of the kitchen are open and empty. The family room, dining room, and living room are lifeless and void. Two large packing boxes stacked on top of each other on a blue area rug linger in the entryway. To the left of the entryway, a carpeted staircase angling to the right waits in anticipation for someone, anyone. At the top, to the left, a bathroom has been cleaned and cleared of all existence of what was once here. Down the long corridor, two rooms with the doors open on each side throw blue streams of light on the unlit area. At the very end of the hall, a closed door is consumed by dark shadows of heavy grays.

The door is white. Faint light from the floor of the room behind this sacred door spills through. Dead light of the day fills the room and taints its surroundings. In the room, a dresser with a mirror attached is home for framed pictures that live on its top. One is of William and Zorah on their wedding day. Three more are arranged in a staggered formation. One is a picture of Zorah, pregnant, with her belly exposed and protruding. Another with the two of them on a boat in the middle of the ocean. The last one is of them in silhouette, holding hands as they watch the sun set upon the world.

Directly across from the dresser, a bed stripped of its sheets sits against the wall below three windows that frame its width. The once-white bed fights off the haunting hue at the head of the mattress. White light beams in a crescent shape in support of the bed's struggle.

'There is still life here."

Blue persistently creeps upon the room and all within it.

"Where is this life?"

"It is here."

The bedroom is quiet and still—so very quiet and still. Blue proceeds in his mission. Suddenly, William bursts through the door of the place that once made him whole. He is unshaven, with his hair grown out on his head and face. He has on a black suit and tie. He loosens the tie and unbuttons his jacket.

He stands in front of the dresser. He glances down at the pictures of them on their wedding day. He looks past himself at the bed in the mirror, then quickly turns and faces the foot of their home, where they live. He puts his hands in his pockets and gazes into the emptiness of what lies in front of him. He closes his eyes to keep alive what lies behind him.

Chapter 3

Zorah and William burst through the door of their home. William carries her in his arms. He places her down gently in front of their wedding bed. White light streams into their windows. The rays of light kiss white, pristine sheets and pillows as Zorah removes her veil from her head and drops it on the bed. She adjusts her white strapless dress and glances up at her groom with bashful eagerness and expectation of this moment.

He begins to loosen his ascot from his tuxedo with confidence and sincerity. He stares at her intensely. The bodice of Zorah's dress and white pearls raise and descend with every breath she takes. William steps towards her. He caresses her right cheek from her lips to her ear. Gently, he cups her face under her chin. She smiles at him. He puts his left hand under the left side of her face and draws her into him. Their gaze becomes feverish with love and desire. Slowly, they kiss.

He moves his hand from her face and glides it down her neck to her shoulders. He makes his way to her back at the top of her dress. His hands find the first entrance to what lies underneath her dress. William unzips her dress as his kisses descend from her neck and shoulders. He kisses the other side of her neck as the dress falls to the floor.

She tears off his coat and shirt. With every removal of clothing, they taste each other and thirst for more. The unbearable pleasure drives Zorah to a state of intuitive compulsion. Wanting to savor this once-in-a-lifetime moment, she pulls away to examine her new partner in life. William does not resist or waive his power. Instead he waits patiently for her return to inflame his ignited passion.

They stand before each other naked and unashamed. She looks unsure.

"What are you thinking over there?" William asks, perplexed.

Zorah hesitates before answering.

"I am as nervous as if this is our first time together. Which is ridiculous because I know it's not. And I…"

"But, it is. As man and wife. As Mr. and Mrs. William Hughes. This is our first time together. We took communion and took vows before God. Everything we were and did alone and individually in this world is washed away. In God's eyes, we were made brand new today. Two people joined as one under one covenant symbolically."

William smiles, "We have yet to pyschically seal this covenant, Mrs. Hughes."

She smiles at him and then looks at the bed. Taking her cue, he moves toward the wedding bed as Zorah follows his lead. William slides between the covers. She does the same, but moves in closer to him. He moves in fast to kiss her. She backs away.

"Deliberate. Everything in this bed from now on is deliberate. No mistakes or mishaps will be created here."

"I agree."

She moves back towards him and kisses him gently. He kisses her back with conviction. He yanks off the sheet that covers them and exposes their nakedness once again.

"Nor covered or hidden," exclaimed William.

The breeze from the sheet produces goose bumps on Zorah's arms. The nipples of her breast harden and protrude. She shivers and rubs her hand against an arm. William grabs both hands and clasps them with his. He brings them to his side and leans in and kisses her. He scans her body in search of the perfect spot. His lips land on her breast and suck in the nipple into his mouth. She squeezes his hand and lets out a sigh. He fondles it in his mouth with his tongue. With each thrust of his mouth, the nipple elongates from the wet sensation. Another part of his anatomy hardens and grows in excitement at the same time.

Zorah's body feels the new contributor to her pleasure speak to her thighs. His warm presence and firm structure render the entrance to her love open and ready for him to enter his new home. A place he soon makes his own as they consummate for the first time as Mr. and Mrs. William Hughes.

Everyone above rejoices as He smiles and says, so be it.

He releases her hands and moves his to her waist, buttocks and then her thighs, up and forward with each thrust. During the heat of their lovemaking, Zorah never takes her eyes off William. With every thrust, her gaze grows intense yet loving—a look of acceptance, faith, and reverence.

William has never seen this look in her eyes before. He stops. She touches his face.

"What's wrong?"

A state of fear comes over William. Fear of expectations that he may not live up to over the course of their lives. Fear of her love and the removal of her love for him in his lifetime. Fear of doubt about him, her, and them. Fear of the ending of this surreal moment between them.

William looks into her eyes, "Promise me that you will always look at me the way that you are now?"

She wraps her long legs around his buttocks, inviting him deeper inside her.

"I promise."

She squeezes down on her legs, pulling them and him towards herself. He fights for control over his thoughts.

"Promise me that you will always fight for us, for this."

"I promise."

She does it again. The pressure of her love begins to break him down in ways that can strip most men from all strength and pride. He unsuccessfully commands his eyes to remain dry and focus.

"Don't ever leave me. I couldn't bear living without you. Promise me."

Trying to regain some type of control of this celestial chaotic moment, William pries her legs from him. With a plea of desperation of reassurance from her, he grabs each thigh with each hand.

"I want…I need to hear you say it."

"I will never leave you."

He releases her legs and falls on top of her as their pelvic walls press together. It seems as if he could not get any closer to her, then he bears down inside her as he pulls her shoulders to him. Zorah body contracts, yet yearns to return to the embrace.

"Tell me you love me." William whispers in her ear as he slightly retracts and pushes again. Zorah moans. William closes his eyes.

"I love you. I will always love you. I will be with you always."

William opens his eyes. He turns from the stripped down bed and stares at the picture on the dresser. Fighting not to look at the bed in the mirror, abruptly, William wipes everything off the dresser. The wedding picture and the others crash to the floor. The picture frames are shattered into pieces as they lay by the door. Several glass fragments are on top of the picture, distorting Zorah and William on their wedding day in its view.

He begins to walk away from the mess he has created. Only able to walk two steps away before he is beckon to return. His eyes gravitate to their wedding picture again. He smiles for the first time in weeks. Wedding day Zorah and William begin to move within the picture frame. They turn towards one another. She straightens his bow tie.

"Thank you."

"You are welcome, Sweetie. There's one thing I want you to always remember."

"What's that?"

"I will always be with you, no matter what comes our way."

They return back to their pose and the picture becomes static once again. William reaches down and begins picking up the broken pieces that have fallen upon and around them.

Chapter 4

Zorah and William are under the covers. She lies on her back between his legs in the middle of his chest. He has his arms wrapped around her breasts, coupling one in his hand. Her right hand reaches around him like a vine coiled around a tree. She strokes his neck and head. He leans to her left, placing his lips towards her ear.

"I wish we could stay like this forever."

Zorah closes her eyes in an attempt to savor the words William has just spoken to her. Longing to hear more of his intoxicating words, she reciprocates with playful taunting as she leans her head towards him like a tree to the sun.

"Forever is a long time."

He pulls her closer to his lips and grabs her firmly around her long mocha torso.

"Not with you. Eternity would be just a mere moment in time when we are together like this."

Zorah opens her eyes, grins, and giggles. She lowers her hand in order to find a way to get closer to this man she now calls husband.

"You say this now, but what about five, ten…"

"Twenty, fifty years; it will always be you, right in here."

He points to his chest where her heart lives. She turns and glances at him pointing to himself and the area of his aim.

"Right there."

She touches his chest.

"Yes, right there."

She lays her ear on his chest and listens to his heart greet her.

Chapter 5

William has a small plastic bag in his hand. His chest is pounding. He is unable to move from the standing position. He knows he must, but he cannot take his eyes off the broken glass on their wedding picture. His chest tightens with pain with each beat. He takes a breath and a gust of thoughts and feeling rush into his head. Choices, memories, mistakes, failures, and regrets; they all begin to suffocate him.

William pulls his headphones from his ear and places them on his laptop as Zorah enters the living room. He approaches Zorah with a smile and tries to kiss her. She rejects the kiss, diverting her attention and affection from him. She walks away, leaving him alone with his anguish.

"…I miss my wife…"

William hovers over her as she sits at her vanity. Their bedroom is brightly lit and the light from the mirror illuminates her face, red cocktail dress, and the room, but not within. White light has no power on her, or them, this night. A flood of emotions crash onto him as he shakes his head in disbelief like a boat against a jagged barrier reef in the midst of a relentless storm. He looks at her in the mirror; she does not acknowledge his reflection. He has felt like this before, but she had promised. In a regrettable instant, he realized he is wrong. This feeling was different. The last times were fear. Fear that this was his fate with her, but she promised. He remembers clearly that sacred day and night. Her words to him haunt him clearly tonight. This – this is pain from the fruition of that fear. He shakes his head again without remedy from this wreckage upon the hull of his heart, which her jagged words and stormy silence has inflicted upon him. He aimlessly searches for her heart in the swirling shadows of this surging sea of somber sentiments.

"…I don't want to send Valentine's with you…"

He looks to her once more for any possible sign of hope. All he finds is disquiet. Zorah shuffles in her chair as she fidgets with a tube of red lipstick she just put on, still refusing once more to meet his gaze. *She promised… She promised me.*

He reaches for her shoulder. She cringes at his touch and closes her eyes.

"...I am going back to work tonight, I have a lot of work to do..."

Zorah slams the lipstick on the table. She gets up and begins to walk away without a single glance.

".... I will be there all night. I will see you in the morning ..."

William tries to kiss Zorah in the living room. She rejects the kiss. Rewinds the image again in his mind. He tries to kiss Zorah in the living room. She rejects the kiss.

"...I miss my wife..."

The door flies open as Zorah races into the bedroom. White light of the day cascades into the steaming room. Like a missile reaching its target, she reaches into the closet and grabs a suitcase. She brings it to the dresser. She sees her wedding picture and scolds herself. She will not deviate from her mission to eradicate. She flings open a dresser drawer, snatches the clothing, and begins tossing it into the suitcase. William rushes in and looks at her as she ignores him.

"...I am sorry. It won't happen again. I love you..."

William is in the kitchen, standing, eating a bowl of cereal while flipping through a magazine, as he does during his usual Saturday morning ritual. Adjacent to him is a wall that leads to the basement door. Zorah storms up the stairs from the door. He turns and greets her with a smile, with a mouth full of cereal. She greets him back with a disdain look. She tries to speak, but is unable to find her voice. The longer she looks at him, the more her rage rises to a boiling point and the huge lump in her throat begins to dissolve each elevated breath. As the shock of his uncovering culminates for her, so does his smile. The words finally come to her while she throws him his cell phone.

"…I hate you…"

Zorah tugs on the lapels of her bathrobe and then begins to twist them around her arm like a security blanket as she sits on the edge of the bathtub in the bathroom. Tears run down her cheeks in silence. William's continuous banging on the door deafens her senses with each blow.

"…Zorah, let me in. Please, let me in…"

William tries to kiss Zorah in the living room. She rejects the kiss.

"…I miss my wife…I miss my wife."

She still loves me. I know it. This love is real. I refuse to have this memory of us to be my hallmark images of our lives together. She still loves me. A love like ours doesn't just die because one of us ceases to…She still loves me. I can still feel it. I can still feel her, feel us.

Blue light slightly fades its tint on his face. William lunges for the glass and begins to pick it up without thought. Once he is finished with the wedding picture, he picks it up. He touches them with admiration. He places it face down on the dresser to the side of him. He starts picking up the glass on the picture of Zorah, half-clothed and stomach exposed while she was pregnant. She loved this picture. It was her favorite of herself; one of his favorites as well.

William grimaces as a sharp stabbing pain shoots through his index finger. He drops the glass that is in his hand onto the picture. As the piece of glass falls, so do droplets of blood from William's finger on Zorah's protruding abdomen. William tries to wipe the blood from the picture. The blood continues to drop from his hand onto her belly. He tries wiping it clean from her, but smudges are left behind. He gives up and walks away to tend to himself.

Chapter 6

White Light engulfs them and everything around Zorah and William as they lay on the white pillow. William's dark chocolate skin accents Zorah's brown mocha skin against the white bedding underneath them. Covers and top layer sheets are dangling off the bed and by the edges of their toes. Both are looking straight up at the ceiling, savoring this moment and envisioning their future together, naked and unashamed. Zorah shuffles herself under his arm as she twists her hair with her finger. He moves closer in as well, smiling at her gesture of infusion of one another. Unsatisfied, she places her right leg on his left one, then begin to caress his left foot with her toes. Content with her new position, she tunes back into the portal to their future on the ceiling.

"William, tell me what our children will look like again?"

William smiles, "Okay."

Their children appear vividly in front of them.

"We will have three. Two boys and one girl."

Two teenage boys with his build. William plays one-on-two basketball with the boys.

A little girl looks on from the side.

Zorah imagines them with him.

Enjoying the guessing game, she asks, "Who looks like me?"

"They all do, especially the girl."

"Is that so?"

"Yes. It will be a walking, talking miniature you. Attitude and everything."

Zorah grins. She thinks of herself as a little girl. Visions of her mom combing her hair fill her mind. How her mother would hum a hymn and gently rake the comb through her strands of hair. Eventually, she would join in with the humming, close her eyes and soak in the lullabies of love. She opens her eyes and now she is combing a little girl's hair. The little girl is humming along with Zorah.

"Then, the boys will be mini versions of you."

"Two more of me. Look out world, two more of me to contend with."

"Lord help us all."

They turn to each other and laugh. He wraps his arms around her back as her arms surround his waist. She closes her eyes to relive the vision of her children.

"I can't wait."

Chapter 7

William is viewing something on a laptop while watching television in the family room. Zorah walks in and turns off the TV.

"Zorah, I'm watching that."

Zorah moves towards him and closes the laptop.

Zorah, what's the deal here?"
"I think I'm pregnant."

Fear comes over his face. He takes the earplugs out of his ears.

"Have you taken a test?"

"No, but my cycle is late."

Zorah becomes worried.

"Okay. We've been here before."

"I can't do this again."

"Come sit."

Zorah attaches herself to him like a parasite to a host. Their legs twist and fuse together as she lays her head on his chest.

"I can't."

"But, we can. We can."

Williams looks up to the heavens.

"Whatever the outcome may be this time, we will get through it."

Zorah buries one side of her face into his chest. She knows she can't do this again. Her heart is breaking at the thought of losing another one. The last two were boys; William's sons that they had talked about for so many years. Since then, each month she prays that her menstruation comes. This time her prayers went unanswered. Now, she must take the dreaded test. A test they once welcomed for good news in their dreams of starting a family. Three pregnancies and seven years later, news of starting a family has evoked new feelings and discerns new meaning.

"If you are, just like the last two times, we will take it day by day."

Zorah begins to cry. William knocks on the door.

"And if I lose this one?"

"I know the last time we said third time's the charm and the same on the fourth one, but maybe this one would be different."

The pregnancy test reads positive. William bangs on the door harder.

"Then, we keep trying. God won't keep letting you get pregnant if you weren't meant to be a mother."

William knew while he was saying the words that it was not what she wanted to hear. Zorah sits on the edge of the bathtub in the bathroom. Tears run down her cheeks in silence. William's continuous banging on the door deafens her senses with each blow.

"Zorah, let me in. Please, let me in."

William and Zorah walk into the house. William has a plant and a plastic hospital bag. Neither dare look at the other. Looking into each other's sorrowful eyes is too much for either one of them to bear.

William heads to the kitchen.

"You want something to drink?"

Without a misstep, he hurries to the sink and turns on the water. Zorah doesn't answer. He grabs a cup from the cabinet to the left of him. A bird in a tree directly outside the kitchen begins to chirp. His hand places the cup under the water. A similar bird in color joins the chirping bird with twigs in its mouth. They start to arrange the twigs into a nest on a branch. William pulls the cup to his mouth and gulps all the water down. Then, he closes the shades to the window.

She goes up the stairs very slowly. By the time she has made it up the stairs, William has joined her once again. As they walk down the hall, the room just to the left of their bedroom is slightly open.

"I think you should get some rest after everything."

Zorah ignores William's plea. She enters the bright yellow room with animals, numbers and the alphabet all over the walls. William puts the stuff down and follows her. Zorah touches the baby crib and removes a film of dust. She walks towards a white dresser with a changing table. A teddy bear is sitting upright on top of the dresser with a railroad conductor hat on his head. She picks up the bear.

William awkwardly stands behind her. Not sure what to do with his hands. Should he touch her? Hug her? *We have been here so many times before and I still don't know what to do.* A man should never be this afraid or unsure about touching his wife. How do you fix something that is unfixable like this…again?

"Zorah, you need to rest."

"Seven months. This is the longest I have carried one of our -"

Tears begin to stream down her face. William can feel her heart crack with each tearful breath. How do you fix something like this? He reaches out and touches her shoulder.
"We can try – "

Zorah drops the bear and walks out of the room before he can finish the sentence. William picks up the bear and places it in the crib. He turns off the light and closes the door.

Chapter 8

Blue Light follows him as William turns on the water in the bathroom sink. He rinses the blood from his hand into the sink. Water and blood swirl together in a cyclone in the basin.

Zorah emerges into his head, blowing him a kiss and mouthing the words "I love you." William looks at himself in the mirror with his beard and worn withdrawn face. He looks away from himself and focuses on the part of him going down the bloody cyclone.

Zorah walks into the entry of the house. William is in the living room, reading a book while listening to music on his laptop. He closes the book, removes his headphones from his ears, and places them on his laptop as Zorah enters the living room. He springs up with a smile on his face.

"You're home."

"Yeah."

"It's nine o'clock."

"Yeah."

"I'm starting to think you are trying to avoid me."

"No."

He approaches Zorah and tries to kiss her. She pulls away and rejects the kiss, diverting her attention and affection from him. She walks away, leaving him alone with his anguish.

"I still have more work to do. I will be working all night."

He watches her ascend the staircase to the upper level of the house. William is left in frustration. She never looks at him anymore. No eye contact for months. No intimacy. Not even a kiss on the cheek or a touch on a hand or back. Nothing.

As he sits back down on the couch, he flips open his laptop. He looks at the book beside him on the couch. Instead going back to his book, he diverts his attention back to his laptop and clicks on his business email account. He starts to press the enter button, then stops.

I don't understand how to reach her. I'm hurting, too. How do I fix this? How do I fix the unfixable part of us? I'm lost here. I'm so lost.

He presses enter. An email appears on his screen from a female colleague at work.

Will,

I enjoyed working with you on this project for the past six months. The time we spent in each other's office for lunches and dinners. I like you. You are one of the good ones. Your wife is lucky to have you.

As you know, I lost a kid once. I understand what both of you are going through. If you ever need someone to talk to or be there for you, don't hesitate to contact me. I am here for you, day or night.

Yours,

Lisa Gavin

He finds her number and begins to dial it.

The finger finally stops bleeding, but the cut is deep and it stings when pressure is applied. He finds a towel and witch hazel to clean the wound. He wraps the cut in a bandage, but the throbbing is still present. He takes a pain reliever to get him through the rest of the day and night.

Chapter 9

Lying on her side facing William, Zorah places her right hand under her cheek, propping her head slightly up from the white sheets. No covers on either of them, William sits up erect with his right knee bent upward. She gently runs her hand up and down his thigh instinctively.

"So, after I have borne you all of your children. Then what?"

Puzzled by the question, William asks his own.

"What do you mean?"

"You know…"

He shakes his head in bewilderment. She gives a jovial smile.

"Are you going to dump me for some younger, hotter chick?"

He chuckles and smiles as he shakes his head profusely. He turns to her and looks her in the eye with sheer confidence.

"I would never cheat on you."

Zorah glides her hand from his thigh past his abdomen to his chest. It lands on the spot where her heart lives within him.

"Good. Because if you did, it would break my heart."

Chapter 10

Zorah passes by William in the kitchen on her way to the basement with the basket of clothes in her hand. She walks down the stairs to the brick laundry area. She begins checking pockets and sorting before putting the clothes in the washer. She pulls out William's cell phone. She shakes her head. At that moment, a text comes through on his phone. She scans it and is not pleased at what she reads.

She looks up at the ceiling. The very ceiling that her husband is standing on directly above her. She wonders what other secrets that he's keeping. She contemplates if she wants to continue to see what else is on his phone. Or, should she wants to ignore the messages in her hand. Keep up the illusion that everything is okay. She types in his code to his phone, scans the rest of the messages from this person named Lisa, and William's texts back to her.

Lisa: You are a good man, William. You deserve a good woman by your side that loves you. Don't be afraid of your feelings for me. When we are together everything about it feels right. Don't turn your back on this…us.
10:30am

Lisa: I am available next week. Same time? Same hotel?
Tues. April 10th, 10:00 p.m.

Lisa: I think about you inside me all the time at work, at home, in my bed. When can I see you again?
Thurs. March 29th, 11:30 p.m.

Lisa: I think I'm falling for you.
Mon. March 19th, 11:00 a.m.

Lisa: Looking forward to getting away with you this weekend!
Thurs. March 15th, 4:00 p.m.

Lisa: I have a better idea. Share more later.

Sat. March 3rd, 9:48 a.m.

William: Last night too close for comfort. Office becoming too risky. Your house again?
Sat. March 3rd, 7:12 a.m.

Lisa: My office – 7pm
Fri. March 2nd, 3:17 p.m.

Lisa: in meeting. Glad to hear that. Meet me in my office – 7pm
Mon. February 26th, 1:15 p.m.

William: I want to see you again.
Mon. February 26th, 1:06 p.m.

William: Me, too.
Thurs. February 15th, 8:32 a.m.

Lisa: I enjoyed being with you the other night.
Thurs. February 15th, 8:25 a.m.

Lisa: 2315 Blight Road. See you in one hour!
Wed. February 14th, 7:36 p.m.

William: how bout tonight?
Wed. February 14th, 7:33 p.m.

Lisa: Absolutely. When?
Wed. February 14th, 7:31 p.m.

William: still want to cook for me?
Wed. February 4th, 7:28 p.m.

Lisa: I understand. When you are ready.

Sun. February 4th, 7:36 p.m.

William: Not sure about that.
Sun. February 4th, 7:29 p.m.

Lisa: Great choice of restaurant! Next time, I'll cook.
Sun. February 4th, 7:05 p.m.

William: I see you. Meet you inside.
Sat. February 3rd, 3:27 p.m.

Lisa: I'm parked by the sub shop.
Sat. February 3rd, 3:20 p.m.

William: On my way.
Sat. February 3rd, 3:00 p.m.

Lisa: Me, too. We should do it again.
Mon. January 1ˢᵗ, 5:30 p.m.

William: Great movie and conversation. Really enjoyed myself.
Mon. January 1ˢᵗ, 5:12 p.m.

Lisa: Glad you emailed me. See you at 12:30
Mon. January 1ˢᵗ, 10:12 a.m.

William is in the kitchen standing, eating a bowl of cereal while flipping through a magazine, as he does during his usual Saturday morning ritual. Adjacent to him is a wall that leads to the basement door. Zorah storms up the stairs from the door.

He turns and greets her with a smile with a mouth full of cereal. She gives him a disdainful look.

"What?" he replies to her expression.

She tries to speak, but is unable to find her voice. She looks upwards for strength. Feeling as if her plea went unanswered, Zorah picks up the closest thing to her. She grabs the plastic glass and throws it at him. She misses.

"What is wrong with you?"

The longer she looks at him, the more her rage rises to a boiling point and the huge lump in her throat begins to dissolves each elevated breath. She tilts her head down and closes her eyes, in hopes that will summon the suppressive silence of her voice, but no avail. She scans the room for more objects to throw. She picks up a spoon and slings it at him.

"Why are you throwing things at me? What did I do?"

As the shock of his uncovering culminates for her, so does his confusion. The words finally come to her while she throws him his cell phone.

"I hate you! I never thought I could hate you as much as I do right now!"

"Stop throwing things and talk to me."

She storms off. He reads the text on his phone and races after her.

The door flies open as Zorah races into the bedroom. White light of the day cascades into the steaming room. Like a missile reaching its target, she reaches into the closet and grabs a suitcase. She brings it to the dresser. She sees her wedding picture and scolds herself. She will not deviate from her mission to eradicate. She flings open a dresser drawer, snatches the clothing and begins tossing it into the suitcase. William rushes in and looks at her as she ignores his presence in the room.

"I think you should stay and talk this out."

Zorah looks up.

"Oh, I am not leaving; you are."

William finally notices the drawer she is packing is his. As quickly as the clothes are disappearing from the drawers, he sees how fast his window of opportunity is closing to make her change her mind on this course of action—for him to vacate their home. *Think, think*; he ponders. *What can you possibly say to make her stop this growing seed of hatred between us?*

"I am sorry, it meant nothing to me. It was only sex."

She stops and stares at him.

"I just lost our fourth child six months ago."

"And it's been over a year since we have had sex."

"Sex. Really. Sex. You know if we were to have any chance

to have that last one, I couldn't have sex."

"What about after? I miss my wife."

He moves towards her to touch her. She pulls away.

"Look, I don't have time for you right now. Give me my spa–"

With the open palm of his hand, William turns and hits the wall several times directly behind him. "See! And that is what I am talking about! My own wife won't let me hold her! My wife!"

Zorah shakes her head and continues to pack.

"Excuse me for how I choose to mourn."

"You don't think I'm not hurting, Zorah?"

"Obviously, you are not. You want to hop back in bed and see if we can produce another lifeless child. And why should it matter to you? You don't carry it. You just make it."

"Wow. So, that is what you think of me. Your portrayal is wrong. I do care. I am hurting. They were my kids, too. The one person who knows exactly how I feel wants nothing to do with me. And that hurt is killing me and killing us."

Zorah stops packing and looks up at him with huge water droplets in her eyes that she refuses to release.

With his own tears in his eyes, William says, "I didn't want her. I needed you. But – but, you refuse to need me. And this pain. It is just too much to bear alone. And – And, I needed someone, Zorah. I needed someone."

Fighting not to understand his side, she tightens her jaw to perpetuate the dwindling anger within her.

"My heart is already breaking, William. Here you go stomping on it and shattering it into millions of pieces. How are we supposed to fix this now? How?!"

No. No. We begin to pray that he say something, do something. He does not. What could he possibly say to that? He has nothing. He feels like nothing. He knows he would be nothing without her. Confused about what to do next, he looks off in defeat in trying to get her to stay.

Zorah begins to walk off, "Pack your own damn self and get the hell out of my house."

Zorah tries to race pass William to leave the room, but he grabs her. She struggles to break free from his grasp. Finally, victorious in the struggle to keep her, he turns her outward and holds her tightly. His chest is press tightly against her back with his face side by side against her cheek. His hands are holding hers in place around her waist.

"Get off me! William, get off me!"

"You gonna stay and work this out with me."

Zorah fights to break free and ends up making them both fall backwards onto the bed.

Zorah is lying flat on her back against the white pillows and sheets. William lies on his side facing towards Zorah and playing with her hair.

"What about you?"

Zorah tilts her head to him.

"In regards to?"

"You leaving me."

"My heart is chained to your soul. Even if I had the

strength to break free, I couldn't. Even if it meant pain and heartache for myself, I won't because I love you."

Zorah breaks free and turns to him. She slaps him. She continues to hit him. He moves closer towards her with his hands by his side, accepting her blows. He buries his face into the right side of her neck. He cries. She slowly stops hitting him and begins to cry, too, reluctantly.

He begins to kiss her on her neck. She grabs his head and runs her fingers down his hair. She hits him again on his back. He grabs her waist and wraps his arms around her tightly. Both of her legs are on the left side of him.

"I'm sorry. Don't leave me. I'm sorry."

She moves her right leg to his right side and raises her knees up to make room for him between her. She relinquishes the grip of her fist and brings her hands to her side. He unbuckles his belt, unbuttons his pants, and pulls them down. She removes the lower half of her clothes from her body, raises her knees up again, and then turns her head to the side.

She lies there, lifeless, as he penetrates her. She closes her eyes in surrender, not to the pleasure of her body, but to the pain of her heart. He tries to look at her eyes. She avoids his gaze. He turns her face toward him, but she looks the other way. He does it again. She avoids him again. He does it for the third time. She looks at him. A look he never wanted to see from her. That dreaded look he feared she would grow to display. He looks away from the coldness in her face and concentrates on the warmth of her internal lower half for the rest of the time he is inside her. Half of her

welcoming him will have to
do for now... for now.

Chapter 11

William lies on her chest as they dissolve into the white sheets of their wedding bed. With one accord, they bask in the silent serenity of this moment. With the sweet embrace of one another, William feels the urge to inject a decree.

"I can't promise you that I won't ever break your heart. I can promise that whatever damage I do, I will spend a thousand lifetimes making it up to you."

Zorah pulls him in closer to her and smiles.

William has a vacuum in his hand. With difficulty, the small handheld device sucks up the small fragments of glass from the floor. He has to work hard to clean up his mess. Some of the glass pieces have stained blood on them – his blood. The picture of them together on their wedding day has chards of glass upon it. He gently brushes over Zorah as they disappear from sight. He turns off the machine and picks up the picture. The images of them, once again, begin to move while in his hand. The two of them are smiling and looking at each other in their wedding clothes.

He smiles at the picture.
They smile back at him. He
begins to shed a tear.

Chapter 12

William and Zorah are lying on the same pillow, facing each other. White light dances around their exposed bodies. Zorah gazes at William's sleeping face. She brushes her hand on his lips. He instinctively kisses it and opens his eyes halfway.

"William, I have another important question to ask you."

"Okay."

"So what if I was no longer a part of your life...what would you do?"

William blinks off the drowsiness of his slumber.

What kind of question is this? Nothing or no one would be able to tear them apart. He wants to sleep in her arms and embrace this moment for as long as they can with good, positive thoughts and completely disregard this notion. Yet, he feels he must answer to her satisfaction. He grabs her hand.

"You will always be in my life."

She was not satisfied.

"I know, but what if it was by some unforeseen tragic circumstance. What would you do?"

Clueless about what to say to her, he begins with a lighter approach.

"That's easy. I would be the captain of my own ship."

Zorah throws a faint smile and a doubtful look his way. "You would be a fisherman."

"No, I would be the captain. Huge difference. You?"

Realizing that she was not going to get a straight answer out of him, she replied:

"I don't know."

After ruining his euphoric moment with questions of

gloom, he was not going to let her get away with such a vague declaration of her love for him.

"Fair is fair."

She touches his cheek and begins to caress it. She is more than caressing him. She is tracing his face. Engraining a vivid image of him for her to reflect on when time is hard and lean for them.

"I would work to forget my loss of you."

"I could never do that." He pulls her close to him, to the point that all they can see is each other's eyes. "This right here, what we have, is timeless. It transcends you and me. The love we share is everlasting. It could never be lost or forgotten by the heavens above. This love is too great. Our love is too great."

Zorah pulls his bottom lip into her mouth. She slowly releases it, only to draw it back in to her again and again. He returns the gesture as he rolls on top of her and then inside of her.

Chapter 13

The table is set for two with candles and soft music playing. William is at one end and Zorah at the other. He looks over to her in her plum dress.

"You know you look beautiful tonight."

Zorah gives a bashful grin.

"Thank you very much."

They continue eating. William begins to think about the last time they ate like this in the dining room. They rarely use it or the plates, napkins, silverware, and wine goblets unless it is a very special occasion.

"So when are you going to tell me what this dinner is really about?"

"Soon."

She takes another drink of wine. Like a little boy, his patience is shorter than a worn out pencil. He can no longer wait.

"Our tenth anniversary is six months away."

Zorah knows he is fishing for his answers. She only wishes he could wait a while more until she was ready to share. She loves him. Last thing she wants to do is hurt him. She knows she has no choice, but this choice she did have control over. She wants to do it right. She owes him that much. Maybe some levity would help her build up the strength to tell him what she has decided for her and them.

"And I just had my birthday last month."

"Did I forget my birthday?"

Zorah laughs, "No."

"Good. I don't think I would be able to forgive myself if I did."

Zorah smiles and stares at him. Remembering why she loves him so much. He smiles back. She takes another drink until the glass is empty. She reaches for the wine bottle and pours herself another round of her encouragement potion.

"We have been through a lot in our short married lives together; some good, a lot bad. These last two years have been very good to us."

She takes another drink.

"I want you to know that I forgive you for everything. What's more important, I forgive myself for how I treated you after our last child. I finally realize the reason for not being blessed with children."

"What's going on?"

"I have been seeing a doctor for about two months."

"Zorah, I have made peace that we will not have children."

" I have been seeing an oncologist, William."

A long pause fills the room. He stands up from the table. He paces back and forth from his seat to hers.

"Whatever it is, we can beat it."

"I have a rare strain of lymphoma cancer. It is aggressive and does not response to most interventions."

"My company is self sufficient. "

"They give me three months at the most."

"Cameron is more than capable of taking over my duties and responsibilities on a long-term status."

"William, listen to me, please. The doctor suggests, and I agree, that I should just enjoy the remaining time instead of fighting the inevitable."

William pounds his fist on a table in front of Zorah.

"You think I am going to let you go that easily? No! I do not accept this, Zorah! I will not accept this!"

She jumps from the unexpected outburst. This is not how it was supposed to go. Then again, things in their lives together as man and wife have never gone as they had planned. Why should this moment be any different?

"You don't have a choice! William, you don't have a choice."

He falls to his knees beside her, as if she had shot a hole through her heart that lived inside him. He caves in from the pain, as if he was the one dying. He buries his face into her lap. She holds him intensely.

"We have no choice."

Chapter 14

Zorah and William are under the covers and white satin sheets in their bed. She lies between his legs in the middle of his chest, face up. He has his arms wrapped around her. She has said these words countless times. She will say them countless more, but right now she is compelled to say them fervently.

"I love you."

William smiles as he relishes her declaration.

"I love you."

"No matter what happens, this is us. This bedroom. This moment."

"I know."

Zorah and William are under the blue comforter on their bed. She lies between his legs in the middle of his chest, facing up. He has his arms wrapped around her. Zorah has always been a small woman in size. The cancer has made her a mere frame of fragile and weak bones. The breath of life does not come easily to her. He grabs a damp washcloth and gently pats her forehead. She never wanted him to see her like this. She was always the strong one. She was the rock that would not be moved from this relationship. Or was he?

With a dry mouth and lips, Zorah takes in a big gust of air.

"You are too good to me." He knows her words are sweet, honey lies that he willingly ingests. The consumption of her words has a bittersweet aftertaste. He warns her that he would never let her go without a fight. His silent battle is coming to an end. He is losing his war, his love, his world, and his life. He has failed her. Too many times he has felt this. Too many times he has not lived up to being the husband she deserves.

"I haven't been good enough."

It took everything she had just to say, "Shhhh," and put her hand to his lips to summon him to cease.
 "I don't know how to live life without you."

"I...will...always...be with you."

He holds back his tears and kisses her on top of her head. Then, he remembers their wedding day and their wedding bed. The same bed will now be their deathbed.

She wanted it this way. This was one thing he did not fight her on.

At first, he thought it would taint that special moment and vanquish it from the room. Instead, it is the only thing he can think about for the last few weeks. Each word that was said between her and him, every look on her face on that day, that divine day, is engrained in his mind. Somehow, he believes she does, too. They have been repeating words as if it was a scene from a movie. This last day is no different.

William presses his face against the side of her face and whispers in her ear.

"I wish we could stay like this forever."

Zorah takes one last breath and turns to his chest and rests there.

"Forever…is a…long…time."

Williams says as he has so many times before, "Not with you."

She smiles and listens to his heartbeat and hers stops. She dies and he loses a piece of himself with her.

Chapter 15

Lifeless William stands at the door. He looks back at the bed as White Light dispels the last of Blue Light from it. For a moment, he thought he saw…but it could not be. He turns off the light as he leaves and closes the door behind him.

Celestial images of Zorah and William are in the bed talking, laughing, and holding each other.

"You see, the greatest power in the world and the heavens is love. Love cannot die. There is still life here."

Blue Light reluctantly disappears. White Light, the

heavens, and Love look down
and marvel upon Zorah and
William for all eternity.

www.ingramcontent.com/pod-product-compliance
Lightning Source LLC
Chambersburg PA
CBHW021115130626

46554CB00002B/707